T0164788

Silk Rose

JEREMIAH NICHOLS

AuthorHouse™
1663 Liberty Drive
Bloomington, IN 47403
www.authorhouse.com
Phone: 1-800-839-8640

© 2011 Jeremiah Nichols. All rights reserved.

No part of this book may be reproduced, stored in a retrieval system, or
transmitted by any means without the written permission of the author.

First published by AuthorHouse   4/25/2011

ISBN: 978-1-4567-3973-7 (e)
ISBN: 978-1-4567-3974-4 (dj)
ISBN: 978-1-4567-3975-1 (sc)

Library of Congress Control Number: 2011901878

Printed in the United States of America

Any people depicted in stock imagery provided by Thinkstock are models,
and such images are being used for illustrative purposes only.
Certain stock imagery © Thinkstock.

This book is printed on acid-free paper.

Because of the dynamic nature of the Internet, any web addresses or links contained in
this book may have changed since publication and may no longer be valid. The views
expressed in this work are solely those of the author and do not necessarily reflect the
views of the publisher, and the publisher hereby disclaims any responsibility for them.

This book is written for and dedicated to my good friend Linda Brady.

Jeremiah Nichols has one amazing daughter Katherine Grace Nichols. His parents are Lee and Paula Nichols and they all reside in Monahans, Texas. Jeremiah is a graduate of Monahans High School in 1996 and he graduated from Texas A&M in 2003 with a Bachelors in Industrial Distribution. While he is not writing books he writes songs, poems, sermons, and sometimes preaches on Wednesday nights at Grace Fellowship Church in Monahans.

I would like to thank God for everything, my savior Jesus Christ,

Special thanks go out to my family: my beautiful, amazing daughter Katherine Grace Nichols, inspirational and loving parents Mom and Dad Nichols, wise Uncle Dexter Nichols, Aunt Kathy Nichols, Lexie, Caleb, Judy, and Scott Nichols, sister Leah Nichols Cavitt, John Cavitt and the boys Shepard Jamison Robert and Regan Cavitt, sister Alyson Myers and all of the Myers family, Aunt Bonnie and Uncle Orville, Bryan and Billy Kidd, Kathy Hannah and Keith Norris, Kelsy Aaron and the new baby Brown, Chyenne Cody Norris. Lorrie and Donna Tramell and their families, Joan Dye Christopher, Wayne, Michael, Star and the Duncans.

I would also like to thank the following people for being such a good friend: my amazing pastor Mark Bristow, you and I put the we in awesome Lisa Bristow, listener Ron Long, friends the Carrells, hilarious Eddie Day, very funny visionary Chuck Rogers, jokester Sid Scarboro, Rueben Browning, Peyton Beard Ashley, Billy Beard and his family, Dianna and Wendel Harkey, Joe and Lana Flores, Holly Harkey Beggs and Jonathan and Kennedy, Jackie Jeffery and Judy Harkey, the Woody's, Zeke Dawdy and the Dawdy's. Matt Wittie and his family, Marcos Sanchez my neighbor, Becky Calder my other neighbor, The Dendy's, The Bean's,, Amber and Hannah Benad, JoClare McCurdy, Brandon and Gail Wade, Melinda and Melissa Wade, Misty Mayhall, Paige White, Paige Tamplin, Jenn and Jeramy Montgomery and the Monty's, Sandra and Wally Meeks, Becca Curtis Terry and Steve Steen, Jennifer and Jeremy Jacob, Connie and Jake Jacob, the Dewey's, Sabrina Chase and Elizabeth McAdams, Don and AnnaRae Brown, Wanda Lemons, Everitt Hewett,, The Nussey's, Waylon Wilcox and all of the Wilcox's, Tregg Passmore and all of the Passmore's, Jon, Leeland, and Big Ed Day, all of the Collins' family, Kathy Mike Shelby and the Corneilieus family, Sammy and Zain Carrell, Matt Sammy and Sarah Carrell, Roy and Zeida Young and all of the Young's, Big Phillip, Amy, Phillip, Jay (we will see you someday), and Brandon Bell, Shannon Huckabee, Ryan and Mark Valenzuela, Keith and Bridgett Bilski, Ana Castillo, Ali Covington, Jami Carter, Jena Tisdale, Cody and all of the Stocktons, Danielle Tyler Brandon and the Lee's, Tres and all of the Thomas's, Miss Jones thank you for all your support, Mrs. Thomas (we will see you someday), The Heinz's, special thanks to Janell and Jay Kelton, Lisa Savage Hack and Denny Savage, Big Denny and Libby Savage, Jason Larissa and the Pittman's, Hector Hernandez, Cheno Sonya and the Navarette's. Ryan Reagan and the Williams', Crystal Swenson, Kelley Cooke, Abbie Watts Hubbard, Amy Morgan and Nicole and the

Hammonds, Athena Jessica Jenny and Linda Johnson Jerry (we will see you someday) Dustin Johnson, Bianca Watson Foley, Melissa Allen, Chad and Heidi Branham, Chris Morris, Lilly and Gatan Patel, Scott and Tonya Taylor, Debbie Coffee, Regina Fuentez, Regina Juan and the Popaleo's, Michael Philbrick, Jesse Bejaran, Michael and Laura Defranco, Coach Ward, Mark Moore, Coach Moore, Coach Cliff, Tonya, and Mrs Gardner, Coach and Mrs. Curry, The Weavers, Coach Curley, The Teinerts, Kevin and the Swanners, Will Karen and the Kempers.

Silk Rose

INTRODUCTION

The internet was a paramount facet of every single woman's life during the beginning of the century. Posts of an intricate nature were sponsored on every matchmaking site of the early century. Matchmate.com was the ideal site for any single woman in the US seeking, an also single attractive male counterpart, for a long since deserved romance, that could not be found in any realistic setting. So therefore Matchmate.com allowed males and females, attractive, and of the same type of nature to post their profiles, so that other single individuals could potentially find their soul mate. Realistically speaking this was a phenomenon that occurred only once in a blue moon. To actually find your realistic soul mate on an internet site is a feat that was actually unheard of during the early part of the 21st Century given the limited technology that was extracted from a given matchmaking cupid type of website.

Thus derived was Matchmate.com, an internet site for all single women, that actually could give the hope of someday finding a potential soul mate on the internet. So therefore thousands of somewhat desperate women would log on to the site each day to find a message from; what they hoped to be their eventual and actual soul mate, someone that they could spend the rest of their supernatural life with and actually be happy and satisfied with. Thus began the search of Christie Columbo a recipient of an early mid life crisis that left her with the shattered dream of ever finding a soul mate again. She was the type of women that was experienced in the world and she had once known love but remembered it only as a ghost of her past. To her love was something that she could never achieve again and served to her only as a memory in her earlier years. She felt that she was no longer attractive to members of the opposite sex and that she could possibly never love again.

Christie's search began with an over exaggerated sense of disparity with the best possible wording to put it. Her individual profile began as such: Heartbroken female seeking attractive male. And as such she began her journey from single women, or so should more accurately say desperate single woman, into the ranks of actual counterpart of the opposite sex into single and dating womanhood. Dating, ahh yes, it is a many splendid thing. Wondrous for both individuals until the inevitable happens. Dating it is the most unusual thing really. It happens when two individuals, preferably of the opposite sex decide that they would like to schedule a date in which they both go out to dinner or a movie, and this is not always the case but the most conventional. The two individuals then will decide if they would like to go out on other dates. If they do and have several successful dates and would like to see the other individual again, then somewhere down the road one of them remembers their initial date, and this is mostly the female of the dating party, the male usually could not care about this sort of thing at all. Dating usually ends in either a breakup or with both individuals committing both of their lives to each other for as long as they both should live, although this usually never actually happened and somewhere ends up in yet another breakup.

Christie with such a sincere and innocent heart wanted so desperately to find the man that she was meant to be with for the rest of her life, and all of the conventional methods of finding a man had never worked for her. She had a horrible breakup with Simon Cagney, the man that she once thought was the one. This breakup would leave her scarred for life and totally distorted her viewpoint on the subject of love. She had never loved someone with all of her heart as was the case with Simon. He was such an amazing man that had so many positive qualities that she always thought the world of.

When they were actually dating for the whole four years that they were together she discovered so much about herself that she never thought was possible. She was living the utopian dream then one day everything was just going wrong between her former lover, and the result was devastating to her, the breakup was utterly awful to say the least. As she spiraled down into the depths of despair her grip on reality was fading ever so quickly, the world that she had worked so hard for with her relationship with

Simon was all taken away from her in an instant. Jonah had nothing on this woman it was such a Jonah day that she never thought would happen given the depths of her relationship with her thought to be soul mate and perfect man. She had replayed the events that took place on that ever so dreadful night that she was haunted by what could have been the outcome of her breakup.

She knew that it had to be because of something that she had done or said that brought about this breakup. She had contemplated the possible events that she could have brought about if only she had it all over to do again. She would change so much about that fateful night if only she could have it to do over again. Sadly God does not grant this type of situation during the natural lifetime of a person, she thought that perhaps that in the afterlife when she would make it to heaven that she would someday get the chance to go back and change it all. Then she would know what it was like to be with Simon forever in her lifetime.

They were so close to each other and kept nothing from each other and then in a flash everything that they had both worked for so fervently was taken away from her. After the breakup and the attempt to rebuild her life without him in it she would go out with Angelica and her other friends to meet single men at bars and clubs, but nothing ever became of this type of meeting a man.

Angelica had a friend that had found her husband on the internet and then she told Christie of the possibility of meeting a man on the internet. Christie was totally not interested in meeting a man on the internet in the beginning, but she slowly came around to accept the possibility of meeting someone in this manner. So with what was left of the shattered ruins that was herself, she decided to take Angelica's advice, and post her profile on matchmate.com. Little did she know but this would be a major turning point in her life.

Chapter 1

Eastern Afganhistan Taahbag

Sweat dripped from his alabaster brow onto is sniper rifle as John Private 2nd class tried to get a lock on the target. The target was red shirt General Allabaaz Afghan rebel responsible, to John's knowledge, for 15 deaths, kias, during the past month of the campaign against the US Army. Crouched high above on a mountain overlooking a Talliban camp Sargent John Hill said, "Red shirt confirmed, target, no lock, repeat no lock!"

Spotter Mike Freeman had the vision binocs glued to his eyes, "Red shirt in sight do you confirm?"

"In sight, but no lock on target."

"Do you know what this means to the fight on terror? You have to execute this mission you blind bitch. Is there something wrong with your rifle?"

Screaming in total frustration John says, "In sight, but no lock confirm."

"If you don't get this we are totally screwed, we've already been spotted by their crew you have 30 seconds before he enters the hummer. Do you have a lock?"

John was about to throw his rifle down the mountain, "The freaking scope was not aligned right."

"Who put the scope on the damn rifle?"

" I don't know."

"Don't give me that who did it?"

"Okay, Briggs calibrated this scope before I put it on."

"Great! Now there's no way, and we're running out of time, damn it. Your going to have to fire blind that's our only hope."

"Why did I trust that freaking bastard! That's it!" John takes the whole scope off the rifle and chugs it down the mountain. "Enough of that." He then realigns his eyepiece as the General keeps walking his way, getting closer and closer walking away from the car. "Perfect he's coming our way I am just going to wait."

"Where is the freak going?

"I cant tell, but I have a lock."

"Execute before we lose him."

"Sure thing." Just as a door is opened at the base of the mountain by a gahnner John pulls the trigger.

Chapter 2

RIYADH, SAUDI ARABIA

One day later

Armed Guards watched the cavalcade of cars on the distant dusty caliche horizon approach, as one of the guards said, "Can you hold this for me?" It was a deck of cards, he handed it to the other guard and the guard's hand immediately fell to the floor.

"Hahaha, very funny, you know that there are American TV shows for jokesters like you."

He acted like it was so heavy that he couldn't pick it up. "Give me a hand over here Rhoyak."

"Quick, they are approaching, enough with the silly games, there is a car at the rear that I don't recognize."

"How far back do you think it is?"

"They probably can't see that someone is following them."

"I'll alert the Sheik." He grabbed his walky talky and pressed in the side button that was covered in dust. "Rhyanton you have someone following you back about 100 yards. Should we take them out?"

"Rhoyak, it is my new business partner Mustafa Hasbaland. Who do you think you are 2Pac, no need to go poppin a cap just yet. We will hear his proposal and then I will tell you what to do."

"Yes sir."

"Now let him through."

The other guard heard the entire conversation and was getting anxious. "I want to press the button for the gate."

"No you fool you did it last time."

"It doesn't matter, let me see the thing."

He snatched it out of his hand and ducked and crouched in the corner of the two story watchtower. He peeped his head just over the ledge so he could see when they were arriving. Rhoyak was furious so he tackled Hanchey and pulled him out from the corner and took the box just before the button was pressed.

"You idiot they are not to the gate yet." So he pressed the button and the gate closed. "I have to take a piss, go over here and look over there."

"I am going over here and looking over there." Hanchey said mockingly in a very thick Saudi accent. It was a pretty funny scene as Hanchey got a water bottle and started pouring it out over the ledge on the other side of the tower, acting like he was pissing too.

"Why are you pouring out your water on those poor dogs."

"I'm not."

"Well then what are you doing?"

"I am pouring out your water bottle on those dogs."

"Gosh dang it Hanchey, let me have that."

The two fought for a bit then noticed that the caravan was at the gate with the driver looking up about to radio them. Rhoyak immediately pressed the button and let them in as the gate slid open.

Stretch limo's were in abundance at the palace, mostly Mercedes Benz and some Caddilac's too. The caravan sleeked their way onto the main driveway into the brick circle around the opulent fountain directly in front of the main entrance. All of the members of the board of Terraoil were bailing out of the cars underneath a large portico entrance sided with marble ionic columns. As the main bullet-proof doors swung open the Arabs entered decked out in their custom made turbans and Arabic tailored business suits. The sheik Rhyanton greeted each one as they passed through. The servants showed them the way through to the meeting room.

Sheik Rhyanton's palace was that of opulence and grandeur it was the envy of all of the Arabs in the area and Mustafa Hasbaland had found his way into it through negotiations over the phone and partly through the stock market. They sat at a large oval mahogany table that seated about 15 towel heads, as some of the Americans called them.

The members had the normal chit chat, of what was going to be discussed in the meeting, on their lips as they took their seats. Armed guards were stationed at the entrances with their ammo around their necks and an AK-47 in their hands. The Sheik sat at the head of the table with Mustafa next to him on his right. A huge 100 inch TV screen was playing the local news on the side wall with no volume.

There were Arab drinks and beers littered at each station in front of each member and the Sheik was drinking a glass of ice water to calm his throat before they got the negotiations underway. Next to Mustafa was a ruthless mercenary, Scorda Gamashef, that was his main advocate in dealing with his day to day operations. He had once been a CIA agent and had connections to Langley and could get any intelligence that Mustafa ever needed at his disposal.

Sheik Rhyanton was on his sat-phone and slid it shut and all of the board members were silenced in anticipation. "Members of the board glad you could bring your ugly faces to meet with us here today I know that your wives are not missing them."

They all let out a few chuckles then the Sheik continued. "It has been brought to my attention that my friend Mustafa Hasbaland has been buying many shares of our stock on the exchange. Maybe he wants to join the party that everyone else is missing out on, or maybe he wants to take the party over. Mustafa what is your reason for being here?"

Mustafa had a emerald green turban on with a matching green tie and a full beard and looked the part to take over the company. He was about 5'9" tall and full of vigor and spirit with light complected skin and a silver Rolex on his left wrist. He had a voice that made people listen to what he had to say and now was his turn to deliver his intentions, "I am here not to take you over but to join you. I have amassed a fortune in the Afghan Satellite TV industry and when I see a party of rich ugly talented men I seek only to join the party and maybe bring some soap, that is if you will have me."

The sheik had his elbow on the table and took a sip of cold ice water when he heard this. He adjusted his turban and spoke, "Of course we could always use some extra funds to be brought to the party how much cleaning of the company were you thinking?"

"The soap was only for your ugly faces, I was merely thinking of your unfortunate wives."

"Hahaha." All of the men at the table erupted in laughter.

"I would like just to be a part of the company, a minority stake in Terraoil is my goal. Say 40%."

"Well then, let us set this to a vote and we will see if we decide to accept your offer. Men all in favor say aye."

All of the board members said unanimously, "Aye."

"They have spoken. Welcome to our party."

It was all smiles and laughter around the room as Mustafa's phone started ringing. "You will have to excuse me for a minute."

Mustafa and Scorda stepped outside to talk, it was Osama bin Laden and he had urgent news. "Mustafa, there has been an incident outside of Kabul."

"Yes, what has happened?"

" General Allabaaz has been assassinated by the Americans, I have gathered my men and we are planning an attack."

"What kind of attack?"

"Tomorrow there is a plane leaving New York with a certain person responsible for plans to destroy our network and she must not be allowed to reach her destination."

"I see."

"We will take care of her."

"Do what you must Osama. Allah be with you."

"I am moving my base of operations to a remote location in Somalia I will contact you when everything is set up."

"I am about to sign an agreement to take 40% of Terraoil so everything is going according to our plans. You get the boom and I will get the audience."

"Very good."

"Goodbye."

Mustafa rejoined them men in the meeting room and the Sheik was there with the paperwork already drawn up with a Monte Blanc on the table at his seat.

"I thought that you might reconsider."

"Never, this is my destiny."

He signed the papers and now he was a part of the largest oil company in the world.

The Sheik was very enthused about this new addition to his dynasty and as they shook hands Mustafa could only see the future. "So tell me more about your logistics operations to America. I am very interested."

"Well, I have just completed the manufacturing of a fleet of oil tankers like the world has never seen."

"And when will these tankers be operational?"

He proceeded to tell him all about the new tankers.

Chapter 3

CHRISTIE COLUMBO NYC

God filled with the void that once was love. She had known love once before in the most amazing context. The love that she had was beyond imagination it was the kind of love that only comes around once in a lifetime. The kind of love that connects the heart to their soulmate, the person that you are meant to be with for the rest of your life. This is no ordinary type of love, and she let it slip away, she thought, as she was deciding on what to insert in her biography on matchmate.com.

The type of love that only exists in the heart and lives on for a lifetime. She never thought that she could actually ever find another type of love that could ever compare to the love that she once had. He was beyond amazing and she thought that no one could ever actually fill the void that she once knew as love.

She posted her biography on matchmate.com and then expected no one to actually answer it. Then she found herself deciding on who she should respond to. There were several interesting fellows that she could decide to respond to. She had tons of responses and she was utterly confused at who she should actually respond to in her emails. She then noticed that someone named Alfred Von Monk had asked her a question in an email that demanded her immediate attention.

Alfred had noticed her posting and thought that she was an ideal candidate for a potential friend and possible soulmate, if they actually ever did exist. Alfred then wrote that "I noticed your posting and I thought that we should keep in touch, being that we were both with the same type of personality and we were seeking the same type of relationship. Would you do me the honor of letting me call you?"

Christie then quickly responded to this email that she was interested in meeting this Alfred Von Monk and that "We should schedule a time to meet in person. And sure call me, you might just want to send emails or chat at first though." She was looking forward to her meeting this interesting fellow.

She then decided to ask if he was single and that he had never been married because she had never been married and she was waiting on the right person to devote her life to, if this was the type of love that he was looking for."

Alfred then responded, "I believe that love was written in the stars and thought that if love was meant to be that serendipity would take over with the relationship. The love would eventually find itself again and that we would otherwise meet by some chance happening that was written in the stars, and that we would find the love that we were meant to be with for the rest of our lives. If it was truly meant to be that love would bring us near each other and would guide us together and take over our lives as wet have hoped for."

Christie then thought that if this really was love that brought Alfred and her together on the internet of all places that serendipity would somehow bring them together in some other type of meeting and that they were destined to be together if serendipity would actually bring them together in some other type of meeting other than on the internet. So she responded to his email and requested that they should get together and chat with each other and find out what each other were really like while on the internet.

He replied with an email most hurriedly and said that "I think that, that would be an excellent way to get to know each other and that chatting is an ideal way to get to know someone."

So she then decided to activate her once obsolete instant messaging program and actually use it for a change and respond to Alfred's email. So they scheduled a time that they should meet on the instant messaging program and they then decided that it would be ideal that they should meet on the internet at 9:00 on a Tuesday night which both of them thought that they could schedule an opportune time that would fit both of their schedules.

So they both looked forward to this internet meeting of sorts, and that they were both interested in meeting each other on the internet to determine what each other was like. So as promised Christie then decided that Alfred was the type of guy that she could be potentially interested in. They both had the same personality type and they both had once been in love and they were longing for the type of person that could fill the void that they once knew as love that now only served as a haunting memory, that eclipsed their thoughts of ever finding love again.

Alfred had waited for this type of opportunity for his whole life, or so he thought, as he was reminded of the woman that he once loved and now served only as a type of memory that would forever define the type of woman that he would never find again. Christie Columbo was the exact woman that he had hoped that he would find on the internet and he never dreamed that he could actually meet her. He was satisfied with the internet type of meeting and hoped that chatting would fulfill his dreams.

Christie Columbo was the sort of woman that he fancied that he could actually talk to on the internet unlike all of the other previous attempts at internet relationships.

He then instantly recalled the most recent attempt at love on the internet, and thought that this type of thing would happen again with Christie, so he did not set his expectations too high with Christie. He thought that this would be a good experience for himself that would serve as a reminder that love only happened once in a lifetime and that ever finding love again would be an impossible feat that is unheard of in any internet type of relationship.

Just as promised he did in fact meet her on the chat program at exactly 9:00 on the next Tuesday night that he had available on his schedule. And as such did Christie meet him on the exact time that they had scheduled. She had planned on meeting him for over a week and was very much looking forward to the event.

So she put on her best clothes and readied her camera and angled it directly at her blossoming breasts in the printed get up that she had envisioned. It was a flowered printed shirt that revealed probably too much of her breasts but she thought, "what the heck," she had put on her bio that she was voluptuous and was seeking a man that could admire her beauty.

Alfred was just the sort of guy that didn't take all of the bio so seriously and he thought that what she had put on her bio was just another way of trying to find the right guy, no matter what it takes, even if it meant exaggerating her breast size on her bio. But soon he would find out the truth about her blossoming breasts, and yes they were definitely blossoming to say the least, for soon he would find out exactly how voluptuous they were.

However, she might have planned this too perfectly for Alfred had a soft spot for a beautiful woman with brilliant breasts. So was it a stroke of genius to point the camera directly at her breasts, that is all that really matters, however Alfred was not the sort of guy that focused too much on the asthetic appeal of a woman he was very much more interested in exactly how the woman could make him feel about himself. He was soon to find out that Christie had the appeal of a very attractive woman that could tempt him in more ways than one. So thus began the conversation that Alfred was about to embark upon.

He types, "So how are you Christie?"

She so very patiently replied as a beautiful woman would do as such with the normal greeting of, "Well Alfred I am doing just fine and I hope that you are doing as good as I am right now, because I have been looking forward to this as long as I could remember scheduling the conversation. I definitely remember the anticipation that I experienced when scheduling the event."

Alfred responded with an emphatic, "Well, Christie, I am very pleased to hear it and I, as well, have very much anticipated this event and have several interesting questions for you and I hope that you have anticipated the same response that I have anticipated."

She very cogently replied with a somewhat foretastedly response in the as such manner, "Alfred your words come as honey to my ears and your intentions are very meaningful, in your rather reluctantly manner to discuss exactly what you are here to discuss, so I must start the interrogations with the question of so have you ever been in love?"

He soon replied with an emphatic answer of, "Well yes, Christie, I have actually been in love at some point in my rather bleak lifetime and it was the love of a lifetime that I cherish rather dearly to this day I think of her very often even though we broke up in a rather abrasive manner several years ago."

She then promptly replied with a very embracing and comforting reply, "Well, Alfred, I hope that she was everything that I know you deserve in a woman and everything that you could ever hope for, even though that you are currently not still seeing her. That, however, is very fortunate for myself though in the fact that I am currently seeking a rather suitable counterpart to my humorous self, in the not so serious sort of way. I know that you most definitely deserve the best in any woman and I hope that someday that I will prove to you that I am the sort of woman that you could possibly fall in love with."

She continued, "I am sorry, I am getting ahead of myself now, in all of that, I am sure assumed nonsense with the aspect of love on the horizon. I am sure that love in a woman is not really an issue with you as long as she is in the attractive sort of nature to you, and assuming this I hope that you will learn to find myself attractive, in any sense of the word."

Alfred was rather pleased with her reply and he soon replied with his own response, "Well, yes, Christie, I do most certainly find you attractive in every sense of the word and I think that I could potentially develop feelings for you in the near future and I hope that this does not come as a surprise to you because I have always had a natural instinct about you from the very first email that you sent me."

Christie very said with emphasis, "Alfred, I am sure that all of the women that you talk to find you just as attractive as I do and I am sure that you know exactly how to impress a woman with you very articulate manner of speaking to a very compassionate woman such as myself. So I have to develop this conversation a little further and ask you to tell me exactly what love was like for you, with this rather fortunate woman that shared your love."

This was exactly the sort of questioning that he loved to elaborate upon to a potential suitor of the opposite sex in knowing that he could possibly extend his romantic appeal in his description of his love for his ex girlfriend. "I am very pleased I must add to your line of questioning and I very much welcome a reply however, I must warn you of the intense nature of the reply that I am about to give you to your very suitable question for the start of a potential relationship, I however, do not mean to rush things with this reply though in the fact that I already find you a very capable potential soulmate to say the least of expressing my feelings for you."

He continued, "So, as such, I will begin my response, I must admit that such as this relationship began it was love at first meeting and I felt that she was my potential soulmate for the rest of my rather uneventful life from the very second that I laid eyes on her. From the very beginning I had a sense about her that she was the one that I could spend the rest of my life with, somehow I knew that she was the one. The very one that could delight the very fiber of my being. From the way that she responded to my question of what was her name she had a somewhat of a air of her being that resonated from her soul that she was a magnificent person that

I could love for the rest of my longing life. Love at first sight? Yeah you could definitely say that. There was a definite attraction there."

"She answered all of my questions with a answer that I could only dream of in a manner that was so attractive to her very nature that made me want to kiss her from the very inflections of her speech that made me want to hold her and never let go. She was my dream come true she was everything that I could ever want in a woman and she made me feel so good about myself that I just wanted to thank her for even speaking to me. I was not worthy of the very conversation that we were having and that I owed her so much for the way that she made me feel that I knew that no one had never made me feel before, that she had something about her that made me want to never let go of our conversation."

"She was everything that I had never imagined that I could possibly dream of, she was everything that I had ever thought that love should be like. I could never have imagined that was possible that I could have found my potential soulmate. The very fiber of my being resonated from my very soul that made me want to shout for joy that made me want to scream it at the top of my lungs that I had finally found the one that could make me happy for the rest of my life."

"How could I have been so lucky to find an angel such as this she made me feel that I ws an undeserving King of a very suitable Queen. How could all of this be? How could I feel this incredible about someone that I barely know? I want to know so deeply that I long to long for that my very being could have never have imagined was possible in a woman. She was every man's dream in a woman and I felt that I was the luckiest man on the face of the Earth to even have the delight of talking to her. Who was I to have this undeserved privilege of speaking with an angel from heaven."

"I wondered if this was some sort of dream and I felt the urge to pinch myself to make sure that all of these feelings were really real. I wanted to make sure that I was not in some sort of luxury undeserved dream that was all a part of my imagination. If this was an actual dream I knew that I was the luckiest man on the earth to actually conceive an angel such as this."

"So I hesitantly pinched myself to make sure that his was not just a part of my dreamlife that I had all imagined in my head and the result was definitely to my liking to my very delight and I found out that this angel was really real and that she actually did exist and that I had to be the luckiest man on the face of the earth to actually be talking to this amazing creature. It was part of God's divine invention that was put on this earth for the sole purpose of making me feel that I was actually worth something, that I could someday find love in another being on this earth and that was not alone in the universe as I had for so long imagined."

"Well I am really going on about our meeting and I am not giving you a chance to get a word in and I am sorry for that but, this is exactly how she made me feel and this is exactly how you are making me feel, to an even greater degree at this very second, in your actual benevolence of granting me the pleasure of actually speaking to someone of your grand nature. I am so pleased with our conversation that I now have to thank you for the very chance of affording me the opportunity of speaking my mind with something of your amazing stature. So please grace me with you angelic words of wisdom. I am longing to hear your opinion on the topic of discussion."

This was most certainly a lot for someone to take all in, She so longed to actually see him in all of his intelligent resounding glory how she had longed for a conversation of this delicate nature. The subject was going exactly as she could have never dreamed of so, that was a definite positive for the romanticist that Alfred had appeared to be that he had so articulately revealed about his very passionate sort of nature.

How was it that she was in the conversation of a lifetime and all she could think of was how he made her feel about herself and how she just wanted to thank him for the opportunity of getting the chance happening of actually getting to chat with a man of his intimate nature and loving demeanor. He was so sensitive how could someone of the opposite sex know exactly how it feels to want to know someone so passionately so intensely so intimately that your very being resonated the love that you felt for him.

This, she thought had to be too good to be true and she was so undeserving of the very opportunity to speak with someone of his sensitive nature. She knew that this could definitely and potentially be the soulmate that she had always longed for and that she thought that she could never actually find, this all couldn't be true she had to be dreaming so reminiscent of Alfred in the earlier occurrence she just had to pinch herself and make for certain that she was indeed not dreaming and this had to be real even though her mind told her otherwise.

So indeed she did pinch herself, and rather hard just to be certain that this new found love was not all in her imagination. Her pinch revealed a side of her that she never though she was capable of and she was very reluctant to reveal her great surprise, to her astonishment, she found out exactly what she only could have dreamed of, and this was not indeed a dream and that Alfred was in fact a real person.

She had by chance with that fate of the gods intervening she somehow thought that this meeting had a divine nature and that there was a greater power at work in the very essence of the direction of their conversation so with all of this to consider she then so methodically replied in the most sincere sort of nature, about her in the most humble of beginnings to the start of a new direction that she wanted to take with this ever so romantic start of a conversation and uttered the very essence of her being with some very simple words of wisdom.

"Alfred, this all comes as some sort of reminiscent dream that I never thought was possible, you are everything that I could ever hope for in a potential soul-mate and I think that this conversation has the potential to reveal a great amount of our very soul, with the very intricate and sensitive nature that you have so willingly revealed about your, so attractive self. It so fascinates me that I want some time to take all of this in before I go making any rash decisions about the potential that I see happening between these feelings that I know that are possible between the two of us. So with the most humility that I can possibly muster I have got to ask you the question that I have been longing to ask someone so here it goes. Please tell me the potential that you see between us, you and I."

He must have been the inspiration to ask such a bold question. She already knew that he could potentially be the one, and that he somehow always managed to bring out the very best in her. If this conversation continued in the manner that she had hoped for that he would always bring out the best in her the very essence of the fiber of her soul that wanted to be felt by her innermost desire so badly.

This was exactly what she could have never had the audacity to hope for in a man. So with this rather bold question that Alfred found rather intriguing he most emphatically responded in an emotion that he didn't know that he was capable of possessing. She brought out the very side of him that Lisa Lacey could have ever hoped to bring out in himself, it revealed some part of him that he never knew that he possessed. So trying not to get too ahead of the emotions that he knew that he was already feeling for this angelic creature in Christie Columbo, he very reflectingly responded with the very essence that he didnt know was possible.

"Christie, don't go underestimating the power that the potential that love could have between two people such as ourselves. More than I could ever hope for in someone I know that I could develop feelings for you and

I believe that I already have. Our future? I think that only God knows what that has for us. As for my feelings on the subject, I think that if we take it slow for a while, you know, only talking everyday and seeing each other as much as we can would just be great."

He continued, "You are so beautiful I do not see how I could possibly keep from wanting you if we were to actually go out on a date. If you wanted to take it slow I would respect that, but for me? Taking it slow means just not moving in together after the first week. Let's just get to know each other and find out what God has in store for us."

She was rather surprised by his candid nature in his direction of the conversation in revealing the potential feeling that he could have for her. She found this ever so attractive and wanted to be close to him and hold him ever so dearly, and knew that this passion that she had already felt for him was more real than any emotion that she had ever felt before. How was it that some beautiful being could ever so graciously reveal so much about himself to her that she knew this was the beginning of a beautiful relationship. This had the caliber of romanticisim that she only dreamed about when she was with Simon Cagney.

Alfred was everything that Simon only dreamed that he could want to be for Christie. So with the most anticipated response that she had ever experienced she gave the reply of a lover that longed for the return of affection that she so deeply felt for Alfred.

"Alfred you cannot begin to imagine the feelings that I have already developed for you in this conversation and I do not deserve to win your affection in any sense of the word and could only dream of potentially hoping for the return of affection that is only discussed in movies. That are the subject of conversation in every woman to woman conversation that only reveals the deepest desires of a woman. And, why am I so willing to reveal these feelings that I have already developed for you in such a new and adventurous embarking of a potential relationship? Well, I will tell you, with the utmost sincerity that I have the most intimate sort of intentions to continue this sensitive conversation and I can only imagine what it would be like to be loved by you ever so deeply and passionately so completely so thoroughly so undeserving."

As if you thought this couldn't get any more sappy she continued, "How I wonder, could anyone deserve the incredible affection that you are so intimately connected to deliver to a being that could never hope to deserve the intimate closeness that you possess. So I am so ever passionately intrigued to ask the bold question of something that I have just got to know about you. So here goes, and I hope the results are everything that I know that they will be. Tell me Alfred what are you looking for in a woman right now at this very second?"

Alfred wanted to reveal his developing and true feelings for Christie. So he very anxiously found the courage to reveal his most intimate feelings for this new relationship that he knew had the promise of something he had ever so had wanted but never found the ability to actually think that he could ever find this type of feelings so early in the relationship. So with all of his heart and with all of his might he imagined the very outcome that he knew would delight Christie in her innermost feelings for someone so undeserving of the very conversation that they were actually having so he then replied ever so sincerely and softly.

"Christie, you are everything that I could ever hope to dream of in a woman you are the very essence of everything that could motivate me to be the man that I know that I could become for you. So in the most simple answer all I have to say is you, you are all that I am looking for in a woman. I am so looking forward to the opportunity to get to know you even better than I could hope to."

She was ever so thrilled to find his reply so appealing and intriguing, she could definitely get used to this sort of affection, this romantic articulation that could only be possible by someone that had the experience of a well versed individual in the very nature of the word love. Oh how she had longed for the conversation that she was actually having with Afred, inspiration was not the word that could most articulate her feeling for this romantic stranger that had serendipitously wondered into her life. She thought that only Simon was capable of making her feel the way that she was feeling at his very second so she with all of her innermost desires expressed something to Alfred something that she only thought was capable with the once distant and haunting love of her life in Simon Cagney the man that she knew was the one for her.

So she then, so softly and intimately, replied, "Alfred what do you think about love?"

"Christie that is a question that I could not answer if it were not for the feelings that I am currently enthralled with by your very presence. You inspire me to be the man that I only dreamed that I could never become so then how could I respond with an answer that would fulfill my truest feelings for the direction that I want this conversation to take. How then could I be so sincere to respond with an answer that I am so overwhelming feeling at this very second. Every notion that I have ever felt about the word love could not begin to describe the feelings that I know that I could have for you. So then am I for or against love? That is the question. I am against love if I could possibly think that I could ever express the feelings that I have for you at this very moment and I will attempt to tell you why."

Was there more to this guy? Yes, he continued, "I believe that love true love only comes around once in a lifetime and that I have already been eclipsed by a love that has been haunting me ever since the moment that I relinquished my feelings for Lisa. This haunting is more that any feeling than I have ever felt before, it is so dramatic that I could never hope to ever feel that way again. How could something so perfect and sacred vanish from my very sight in such a ghostlike way that would change my very concept of the word love. You could not begin to imagine the feelings that have overtaken my imagination since she left my life. How could something so meant to be, so destined to be forever, ever vanish and never reveal itself again."

Yeah, he continues, "I am forever haunted by the wisdom that we shared the nature of our relationship was so intimate so sensitive that I could never imagine to ever feel that way again about someone. I was so into our relationship that I lost my bearing on reality, I did not know where I began and where she ended. We were one being we were one in the same. With her ever so abrupt departure I lost myself in what I wanted to be forever."

"The word forever should actually mean forever, it should never conceive of a notion that experienced the probability that it could mean something other than the definition of the word. I believe that true love should be forever and that it should never consider any other notion that could end up in anything other than eternity. Somehow the perfection of our love found a way to not mean forever, it found a way to separate the being that I had become in her. The unification that had become our very essence had somehow found a way to slip from our grasp on the nature of our love for each other."

Does his previous relationship get any sadder? Yes, he continues, "How could something so perfect have such an ending as the departure of our hold on our unified reality that only existed in the undying bounds of love. This violated the very definition of forever the very definition of what love should be. So could I ever imagine a life where love was true to me again? How can love be true with such a tragic of an outcome of the breakup that I experienced. I can only hope that there does exist a world where love does mean forever and eternity and the unification of souls is really accomplished in the embarking on a journey of a lifetime. So am I for love I cannot say that I am I am for the idea of love I am for the potential that I can only dream of love to be, and I think that there could be the potential possibility in our relationship if forever really meant forever."

She reflected this statement by the thoughts of someone who had once known love herself. She believed that she had actually known love but taking into consideration what Alfred had just said she thought that maybe that there was a love out there that was still waiting to find her a love that she had never known. What was the depth of these simple words that Alfred had just uttered? She was confused as to the potential of the relationship, how could she be so selfish and think of her potential relationship with a man such as Alfred.

She barely knew him but the words that he spoke gave her the idea that she had never really known true love as she had once thought. This speech gave her the idea that true love was something that any human could never attain. How could something so perfect in nature ever depart from the unification of two souls that were destined to be together? The depths of love that he spoke of made her want to cry she had never felt this way before and she wanted to hold on to this feeling forever and to let it go, in every sense of the word.

How could any man ever be so perfect as Alfred, this was beyond her wildest imagination beyond her conception of the word love. This was way too much to take in all at once she needed some time to reflect of the depths of this conversation. She was crying, to her amazement, she yearned to meet this man that spoke of love in such a way as he did. She cried without ever letting him know of her truest feelings. She barely knew this man and already she was experiencing a feeling that she never could of dreamed that she could possess.

Oh how she yearned to get to know this amazing man. She still sobbed a few tears while trying to conceive of a reply that offered such emotion that warranted this discussion of love that she never knew was possible. What could she possibly say that could express her exact feelings at that very second she was speechless and she always had words to speak, but Alfred had left her in a state that she never thought was possible to experience.

The essence of the heart that she wanted to have yearned to continue this conversation with all that was in her. What she needed now was courage, to feel courage, to find the words that could express her feelings, but how could this be done she thought? She did not know she was truly speechless. Her crying did not stop she only felt the words that he had spoken more deeply with every tear. The entity that she had once known as her heart had never felt this way before she had never felt such exhilaration and such juxtaposed emotions so conflicting with her preconceived notion of the word love.

Her heart was torn in a million different directions all at the same time she did not know what she could say that could accurately express every emotion that she was feeling. "Oh, how I want to know this love that you speak of. Oh, how I want to feel this love that you speak of, you must tell me do you think it is possible for me to know a love as deep as you have expressed? You had a lot of good things to say I have to say that I am sorry about your loss of love I am sure that she was an amazing woman, but sometimes the most perfect love just isn't meant to be, if she is the one for you then God will bring her back in your life. I believe in the love that you spoke of, I believe in love forever, I believe in eternity."

She continued, "Alfred you are an incredible person and I cannot wait to get to know you better. You make me remember the love that I once had and how amazing that it was to be in love. So tell me your thoughts on the potential of a relationship between us."

He was distraught he didn't know what to say but then in an abrupt pace around his derelict apartment filled with reminders of his past love he discovered an emotion that he had not experienced in years, and yes it was the answer to all of Christies questions so then with an abrupt pace he regained his composure and sat back down from his anticipating position and delivered what would be his triumphant delivery of a speech that whould establish a relationship with his new found love.

"Christie, in a good way you made me realize exactly how things used to be between my former love that I am compelled to tell you that I emphatically agree that there is a serendipitious connection between us that cannot be avoided that requires immediate attention, that I believe will turn out to be the stepping stone of our epic relationship in all of our future endeavors. So then with no hesitation I will reveal a side of me and my emotions that has not been experienced by myself in so many years that I am compelled to tell you that yes."

"I emphatically agree, that there is a definite connection between you and I and that I cannot avoid the inevitable conclusion that is upon the two of us. I am utterly inspired by your speech of this love that you seek so dearly and I think that there is a potential of unlimited proportions that has been experienced by our chat tonight and I think that we must somehow meet each other to further develop our emotions for each other so with this desperate response."

"I urge you to consider the possibility of potentially meeting me in a very intimate occasion that involves an exchange of raw emotions that will affect the direction for the rest of our lives. But, however, I think that the outcome of the potential meeting of the the two of us will result in an epic love that has not been experienced in my history, so it is imperative that you respond with an emphatic answer. Your heart must agree to that, all of your being must be in agreement with what will otherwise result in the potential misfortune that could befall the two of us that could result in a cataclysmic event. Never knowing if we were meant to be."

Christie was inspired by this somewhat of a speech by the new found love of this utter stranger, that has been the catalyst of an event in her life. It could be potentially dangerous to not consider his heartfelt emotions. It was expressed by his veracious speech, so with all her heart or what was left of it after his conveyance of his past love for Lisa she delivered the speech of a lifetime that would effect her for as long as she will ever be able to remember.

What would be the outcome of a potential meeting between herself and this inspiring man that she had so deliberately began to know as a passion of the soul that had inspired her to be more than she ever thought she could ever be. She was compelled by the holy spirit, she thought, to reply with an inspired answer to his questions, that brought on an utter stirring of the soul within herself that she thought was never conceivable within her rather lack of divine nature and humanity that had driven herself to all of her utter meaningless conclusions. Within the spectrum of what that she thought was so fulfilling that she began to rethink the actual meaning and important consequence of her life. So then in an anticipated answer after she regained her composure she then sat back down in her office chair and conceived of the words that would define her for the rest of her known life.

"Alfred I am so inspired by your presence that you are so utterly able to convey your innermost affections for this utter stranger that you have just began to know. I am so compelled to take you up on your offer of the potential destiny of our new relationship, that I will respond with an emphatic yes, I will agree to meet you in any location and destination that you so desire. I trust your tastes in restaurants and theaters."

She continued, "I cannot stress enough how utterly inspired I am by your outstanding character that I feel that our potential relationship has the possibility to end up in the annuals of love that have never been experienced by any other human up until this moment in time. You have given me the resounding desire to get to know you in a way that I never thought was possible between the opposite sex and I believe that the result will end up with an outcome that will exceed our wildest expectations that we never thought was possible."

She continued, "So with all of my heart I will agree to meet with you with so much anticipation that my brittle heart has never experienced before. So with the world riding on our shoulders when should we devise a time that we could so romantically meet that would have the most profound effect on the two of us?"

Alfred was extremely pleased with her response that he could not contain his emotions and he let out a whoop that could be felt by his neighbors in the adjoining apartments of his building. He was utterly and profoundly affected by this event that he then conceived of an answer that would affect his rather uneventful life up until this second in time. So then he delivered a response that resounded his very fabric of his romantic emotions for this newfound love in his life in a way that could only be explained by the divine angels in heaven.

"Christie I am so compelled to reveal all of my emotions for your at this very moment in time that I cannot find the exact answer to the inevitable question that awaits the two of us so then I will devise a means of communicating that my fragile emotions have never experienced before. I will decide on the most fortunate of conclusions that could ever have the most profound impact on our lives. So would you like to eat at Traccia's?"

Chrsitie was very familiar with this particular restaurant and she had several previous encounters with the place so she was then compelled to agree to this profound meeting that she knew had the possibility of changing her life forever. "Actually I have a close friend that is the owner of Traccia's. I think that it is fate that you actually have heard of this place and I will emphatically agree to the meeting in this rather profoundly romantic venue."

He could not believe himself he had picked the very spot that was so dear to his heart and she actually knew of the establishment. This was definitely fate it had to be so the gods were definitely with him on this so eventful night. He knew that he was in tune with the very nature of Christie in such a way that had made him select a venue that she actually had know of previously. She knows the owner what a divine coincidence this had to be the work of the Lord he thought to himself.

The conversation that they were having, as they got to know each other, better was definitely the stuff of legend in regards to the romantic charisma that the two strangers shared with each other. Alfred was overcome by her intense beauty and her delightful ability to always deliver the right thing to say at exactly the right time. Her questions which were extremely invited gave him a new outlook on his life and gave him an unbridled emotion to want to get to know this amazing woman better even more than his initial reaction. Alfred was glued to the screen as he typed ever so fervently with a plethora of emotions flooding in from all directions at every second that they were chatting.

So with a deep reflection on the intense and revealing nature of the conversation he decided to attempt to give her the compliment of a lifetime. "Christie I have to tell you this before the conversation progresses any further. You have to be the most beautiful person that I have ever met. I am quickly overtaken by a run of emotions that attract myself to you in an ever so romantic way that I have never experienced before. You are more beautiful than I could ever possibly imagine. Your heart is what attracts myself to you so much. You have such a good and sincere heart one of which I once thought that it would never be possible to actually meet someone of your outstanding character. You have the face of an angel from heaven I have been watching you type ever since the conversation began and I am so overwhelmed by your incredible beauty and I am so looking forward to the day that we will actually be able to meet each other."

She was Jarretting she had never received a compliment in such an articulate manner and what was even better than that, was that she felt the exact same way about Alfred. She wanted to find a way that they could meet each other as soon as possible. She was utterly captivated by the words that he typed which revealed a side of himself that she thought that she would never find in another man. Just then she discovered herself starring out the window that was next to her computer desk at the moonlight night that filled the New York skyline.

Suddenly she heard a buzzing noise then it progressed into a flapping type of sound. Something was hovering outside her highrise apartment she couldn't quite make out what the figure looked like but she saw a man clearly in the moonlight that appeared to be hovering right outside of her window. Then in a flash the man was opening her window from the outside. After the window was open the man that was obviously flying with wings and all began to enter her apartment without prior warning.

What exactly was going on she thought she had no explanation for the event. She noticed that the man was carrying a bow and arrow then she thought that she was definitely losing her mind seeing him fly like that and all. Before she got a chance to tell Alfred what was going on inside her apartment something hit her. The man with the bow and arrow had rared back and shot an arrow directly at her heart. She sat there in amazement as the arrow directly struck her in her heart. To her astonishment the impact did not hurt at all she felt no pain whatsoever.

She then began to examine the arrow that was deeply lodged in her heart and decided to pull the arrow out. Just as she was pulling the arrow out she watched the man with wings fly straight out of her apartment window never to return again. So she then pulled the arrow out and found a note attached to the arrow that was not covered in blood as she thought that it would be. The arrow had a message attached to it and it said, "You will fall in love with Alfred von Monk."

She was definitely startled and shocked beyond belief, her emotions had overcome her wildest inhibitions and had seen something truly amazing. As she stood up to take her breath and in a sweeping motion she shoved her office chair back a few feet. She then made her way to the window where she saw the vision to see if the man with wings was still there but much to her dismay he was gone without a trace she had so many questions that she wanted to ask the incredible flying man.

Her main question concerned the note that was attached to the arrow. Somehow with the direction that the conversation was heading she knew that the note was full of many truths. Was she falling for this incredible stranger that had somehow divinely made his was into her life? She couldn't quite say at this point in time so this was the safest position to take considering the depth of the conversation.

For this had the makings of a potential beginning to an amazing relationship. She knew she could have never had this deep of a conversation with her former love Simon, so early into meeting the man. Her emotions had definitely taken control of herself and she had the premonition that this feeling was for real. Alfred was no fluke he was the real thing and she felt lucky that she was the one to find out how amazing this man was, before any other woman had a chance to find his incredible character and integrity.

He was so sincere even more affectionate than Simon had ever been and she hadn't even met this marvelous man that had so quickly taken her heart and sealed her emotions into dying to meet him. Reflecting on what she had just experienced she contemplated on the possibility of telling him about this heavenly encounter. Her eyes were so open to a new vision of love she didn't want to ruin anything that she had just so intensely worked for so she decided not to tell him about it.

If he were not to understand it then the result could be devastating. So then she went with her heart and decided on a time that they could meet. "Thank you so much for the eloquent compliment, it was received with an abounding grace that has delighted my heart. I think that I could definitely get used to these type of articulate compliments. So with that in mind how would 9:00 at Traccia's sound to meet next Wednesday night?"

"That sounds great, I am so looking forward to meeting you. I can only hope that all of our future conversations can be so insightful and delighting as this one has been tonight."

She agreed wholeheartedly as the dynamic chemistry began to sparkle into the late hours in the night. She was so focused on the chat that she forgot to look at him in the screen so to get a better idea of what he looked like she made the webcam go into full screen. Next she gazed into his bright blue eyes and found him to be extremely attractive, she couldn't believe that someone like this would actually be single.

The night began to fade into morning, it was amazing how fast it went by, as they were pouring their fragile hearts out to each other. They both had to be at work early in the morning and they knew that it would be a long day tomorrow, that didnt seem to matter much to either of them. They were so into the conversation trying desperately to learn as much about each other as they could given the limitations of internet communication.

If only this conversation were in person and they were together she could only think of how the night would end. She had a vision of how it would be if they were meeting in person and it made her want to see him even more. It had been years since she had gone out on a date with a man and she was so desperately seeking an intimate encounter with Alfred that she couldnt wait to see him in person. She needed to meet someone and go out on a date so much but all of the other conventional ways never worked into an actual relationship.

Going out to clubs never produced any relationship worthy encounters that were worth scheduling a date with another man that she had met while going out with Angelica and her other friends. Angelica always met men and it always turned up the same results with the men that she had met in a bar or club. She would dance a few dances preferably country music which she was so apt to dance well in the Texas two step. Next she would give the man her number but when they called it was obvious that those type of men were only seeking a physical relationship with her.

Angelica was quite beautiful and always attracted handsome men but they were not the dating or relationship type of gentlemen that she was looking for. Christie would maybe dance a dance or two with some good looking stranger in the country bar but she rarely got a number from a man and never was given the opportunity to give someone her number in return it was not at all because of her asthetic appearance. She was definitely gorgeous, even more so than Angelica was, but she thought that men would never approach her or take interest in her because they thought that a woman of her beautiful nature was far out of their league. So she mostly hung out with the other friends of Angelica while she danced with a variety of other men. It got to the point that she would get severely depressed in even going out to a bar with the girls. She constantly was thinking of how she could get her former love Simon back into her life.

Just when she could not get any more depressed about her love and relationship life there was this amazing man Alfred, and she found him to be so perfect in every way that she was so anticipating meeting him at Traccia's that she decided to offer him her phone number so that they could keep in touch before they were actually going to meet in person. So she then typed her phone number and her intentions into the instant messenger and waited for a response from Alfred.

Once he received the instant message from her he was immediately pleased that she would offer it to him and he agreed that that would be a great idea to keep in touch over the phone before they actually met. Alfred knew of the intimate possibilities that would occur if they were to talk on the phone instead of typing in the instant messenger all night. He then decided to giver her his phone number and told her that she could call him at any time of day that she wanted to talk to him.

Alfred was obviously falling for her and fast he didn't even let Lisa call him at work but he articulated the welcomed call from her at any time of day which also included talking while he was at work. Alfred had been working at TechOne for several years and he had seniority privileges among his boss that allowed him to do his work at any time of day as long as he met his quotas for the week.

He could talk to anyone on the phone as long as it didn't interfere with his work for the company or his weekly programming goals and quota of completion of any specific software that he was working on. "I am so looking forward to hearing your voice on the phone." After typing all night he was interested in actually speaking to her as soon as he could. Alfred then pulled out his wallet and got a pen from his drawer and began to write her phone number down on top of one of his checks and he made sure that her name Christie Columbo was in the neatest handwriting that he could ever sketch. Then he decided to put her into his business Rolodex so that the number in his wallet wouldn't get lost.

He definitely did not want to lose such valuable information as her phone number. Christie then began to write his phone number in her Rolodex as well. Both Alfred and Christie were so enthralled with the nature of the conversation that they both didn't want the night to ever end and could only imagine where the conversation would go if they were to stay up all night chatting with each other and finding out so many things about the other.

They then thought about how sleepy they would be at work if they did actually stay up all night talking with each other. Considering his work that had to be completed the next day he then decided to end the conversation on instant messenger. "I cannot wait to talk to you on the phone and even more I cannot wait to see you next week at Traccia's I cannot remember a time when I have ever been so anxious to meet someone filled with such romantic anticipation."

She then responded, "I know that we both have to be up early to go to work but if you want I would really like to talk with you on the phone tonight if that is okay with you. We don't have to talk very long so that we both can get some sleep tonight before we have to make it to work in the morning."

Alfred took no time to respond and said, "I think that would be a great idea I would love to hear your voice tonight and I think that work doesn't matter to me as much as getting the opportunity to talk with you tonight, so I think if it is alright with you that we could talk as long as you would like to talk tonight or until we both fall asleep on the phone."

Christie then reflected on the work that she was scheduled to complete at Futura tomorrow and somehow as important as her work was to her she also would love to have the opportunity to talk with Alfred on the phone tonight. "I would love to talk with you tonight on the phone and it doesn't matter if I am late to work tomorrow what is more important to me now is getting to know the amazing man that is you."

Chapter 4

The Call NYC

Alfred and Christie

Just then she heard a faint sound of some kind of music in another room in her apartment she thought that it could be her neighbors playing music so late at night. Maybe they were celebrating in some kind of late night party? She wasn't sure one way or the other so she then arose from her chair to find out where the music was coming from. She thought that she heard it coming from the living room, but as she arrived there and put her ear to the wall to check and see if was indeed her neighbors she noticed that all was quiet next door.

She still heard the music though and decided to search the house for any sign of where this music could be coming from. She went to the kitchen and the music began to fade so she knew that it wasn't in the kitchen. It couldn't have been in the living room, the kitchen, or the computer room so she made the conclusion that it had to be coming from her bedroom. She then took a few steps toward it walking from her computer room into the hall where it was ascending into a louder crescendo she knew she was getting closer.

Her bedroom light was off so to get a better idea of where it was located she then turned on the light and the ceiling fan and both came on simultaneously. "Ahh." She said to herself now I can see this is much better than searching for the location of the noise rather than looking in the dark. Her bed was made as it always was, so neat and clean was her bedroom, you couldn't even tell if there was someone living there, everything was arranged in a very nice and neat order. If you couldn't tell she was a perfectionist as Alfred would soon, to his pleasing, find out that she was not only perfect in every was she was also a very organized and neat person.

Alfred always tried to keep his apartment very nice but he never made his bed no matter how early he woke up to go to work. His living room looked like it was not lived in as well, it resembled that of Christie's living room, but with the meticulous organization that only Christie was capable of. He liked to be around organized people he thought that his conversations with neat people were always more interesting than that of a conversation with someone who did not care about how their apartment looked.

His apartment was very neat in all of his other rooms except he never could find the necessity to actually make his bed. He thought that this was such a wast of time he would only get it messed up that night that he slept in it. However, when he knew that he was having company he always made an extra effort to perfectionize his apartment. It had been months since he actually threw a party or social gathering in his pad. If you were to look at his apartment it was obvious that he was indeed a single bachelor.

He had several interesting additions to his apartment over the years such as his flat screen OLED TV that had cost him a fortune since he bought it as soon as it had hit the market and now they were selling for half the price of what he paid for it. OLED means it's organic he is green and all its the only way to be, safe for the environment, better for the consumer. He thought that he could maybe take it back and exchange it for a similar OLED TV that cost much less than what he had paid for it. He watched TV quite often after he would return from work. He was really into sports and liked to go out with the guys at a sports bar to catch an important game that he couldn't get on his cable service at his house.

Most of the time however he would watch all of the sporting events alone in his home dreaming of what it would be like to have a girlfriend over to watch the game with him. He knew that this was not possible to ever find a perfect woman that actually liked to watch sports with him that was what he dreamed of though. He was anxious to find out from Christie if she ever liked to watch sports on TV he knew that the finite probability was not in his favor of ever finding someone as perfect as she was and who liked to watch sports as well. He was very into fantasy leagues on the internet. He would join every fantasy game that was on the internet whether it was basketball, football, or baseball, he even liked the hockey teams that New York had.

What would be the ultimate woman would be someone who would actually go out to Yankee stadium with him when they were having a home game, he would watch any game no matter who was playing. Living in New York his apartment was closer to Yankee Stadium than Shea field and he also liked the Yankees better than the Mets.

He had been to several games at Yankee Stadium with the guys from work but they never went to a Mets game. He did however go to a Mets game several years ago at the Astrodome when the Astros were still playing there. Christie was still searching for the music and noticed a cord leading to her top drawer of her night stand. She walked closer to the night stand and the music got louder, she opened the drawer and found the source of the music it was her phone that was making all of the music.

She then looked at the number and recognized it as Alfred's number so she immediately answered it hoping that he hadn't already hung up as she was looking for the music. "Hello is this Alfred?"

"Yes it is. I hope that you don't mind me calling right now if you want to go to sleep we don't have to talk very long if you don't want to."

"No, no, I am so glad that you called, I am sorry it took so long to answer it I thought that the neighbors were having a party but it was my phone that was making all of the music I forgot where I had put it."

He laughs for a while then lets out a sigh to try and keep himself from making a mistake and laughing too long if she were to take the laugh the wrong way he wasn't sure. He definitely was not laughing at her but rather finding humor in the situation which he was well known to do with all of his friends. He then asks her, "So if you don't mind me asking what ring tone do you have on your phone?"

She was obviously not offended by his laughter and she joined in with a quick laugh for herself then answers his question, "George Strait, All my Ex'es."

Alfred then gathers his composure and says in his trademark deep voice "So I take it that you listen to country music?"

He thought after he had said it that maybe she didn't want to hear about his ex girlfriend so early in the relationship. He knew that some women did not like it when he would speak of his ex. She says in her positive and excited voice, "Yes I love country music but I have never had someone that would actually sing for me. Simon didn't like country music and he certainly wouldn't ever sing for me at all. Once we get to know each other better I would really like to hear you sing, have you ever been in a chior?"

Ever so deeply he responded, "I would love to sing for you sometime, you pick the song and I will sing it for you, I know a lot of country music songs, and yes I used to be in choir at Harvard."

She didnt hesitate and said, "Wow, I am impressed with you going to Harvard and you sing you get even better every time you speak, what was your major?"

"Computer Science."

"Really? and what kind of job do you have now?"

"Right now I am a programmer for TechOne software."

"Really? I am again impressed I know that they only hire the best of the best in your field so you must be pretty good at programming."

"Well I am definitely not one to brag but I have succeeded at every project that they have given me. So where did you go to College?"

"I went to MIT and graduated with a bachelors of science in Bio Chemistry and I got my masters at Yale in Bio Chemistry."

"MIT and Yale wow you must be very intelligent."

Christie says, "You graduated from Harvard in Computer Science I am sure that your IQ is quite high, I can tell that you went to a good University by the way you articulate yourself so eloquently."

Alfred goes, "Why thank you that was a very nice compliment."

Then Christie replies "I could never compete with your amazing compliments that you gave me when we were chatting, you are so amazing with words. So do you give these articulate compliments to every woman that you meet? It definitely swept me off my feet."

Alfred felt a positive emotion as if he had just done something right in complimenting her, "I only give compliments to the most incredible and amazing women that I meet and I can say that I have never met anyone as beautiful or incredible as you."

Christie was flattered to say the least, "Wow speaking like that I dont see how you have remained single for so long."

Alfred then said, "I only give compliments like that to women that I have feelings for, or that I know that I could potentially have feelings for."

Christie then responds, "Well what do you think about the potential between you and I? Before you answer that I have to establish my feelings and let you know in a sense I feel that there is an undeniable connection and chemistry between us I have never shared such passion with someone in all of my life and I can only pray that you feel the same way about me so now could you answer my intriguing question that I am in such anticipation to hear your opinion on the subject."

Alfred then responds, "I hope that you will find my answer as appealing as the question that you have just asked myself. So now to answer your question I enthusiastically will respond with an inspired yes I have the exact same feelings about you that you have about me and I think that most absolutely that I believe that there is a significant connection between us. Our conversation has taken a path that I thought that I would ever feel again. And to elaborate on this specific emotion I feel more positive emotions about the potential relationship that we could possibly share with each other than I have ever felt with the previous loves in my life. I have never had such a romantic connection from the beginning of a possible relationship than I have felt with you tonight."

He continued, "I am overwhelmed in the desire to get to know you and I am just saddened by the situation that is before us that it will be a whole week before we can actually meet each other. I am saddened with such anxiety and anticipation that I cannot to wait one more day to talk to you again so now I will ask you if you think that in your schedule this week that you could possibly find some time to include me in it in any manner that you so desire. Be it chatting on instant messenger or on the phone or even through email I would be ever so pleased to speak with you in the following week in any manner that you so wish.."

Christie then responds talking into the phone, "Alfred I could never be so anxious to hear your amazing voice on the other end of the phone line so yes I think that I would love to hear from you in the following week at any time that you so feel is convenient to you so you can call me any time that you want and I will so be anticipating you phone call or in any other means that you feel that you would like to speak with me."

Alfred was ever so pleased, "Well then can we consider our next encounter a date before the main date next week and I will plan on calling you tomorrow night if you are not too busy with anything."

Christie felt the same intense emotion and she responded, "Well then I will be ever so inspired to hear from you tomorrow night and I would like to consider it a phone date so that we can answer each others question that we have about each other, I don't know about you but I am so excited about this continuing opportunity to get to learn more about you, so a date it is, any time after work tomorrow I will be available to speak with you until the late hours of the night just as we are speaking so late tonight. It is already

2:00 over here and I think that with all that we have discovered about each other tonight that we will have the most excellent dreams tonight so I would like to thank you for the opportunity to get to know you tonight and I will so be looking forward to hearing from you tomorrow night."

"Yeah, sweet dreams Christie, this has really been so amazing, you are amazing and incredible thank you so much for the opportunity to talk tonight. Looking forward to tomorrow."

"Sweet dreams, goodbye."

"Goodbye."

Chapter 5

New York City Down town Manhattan

His bachelor pad was silent, well as silent as could be living in downtown New York. Alfred was fast asleep and dreaming as the constant flood of traffic noise poured in from outside. This didn't bother him at all he was obviously caught up in another wonderful dream. There was nothing that he liked more than to dream, nothing was more entertaining to him than a good dream. Sure he liked to watch movies every now and then, but nothing could compare to a good dream.

Suddenly the alarm clock buzzed and it was time for him to awake and get ready for another day at work. As he stammered out of bed he scurried to the computer to check his email. "Dang it," he said out loud, another day and nothing from Christie, what was going on. It had been almost a week and nothing not a call not an email this was totally unlike her something had to be wrong or he would have heard from her by now. He was beginning to think that he must have said something wrong when they had met there could be no other explanation for her not to keep in contact like this.

He decided to get ready for work and forget about it as he tried to remember as much as he could of the dream that he had just had. On his way out the door he ran into Mrs. Breaston as they exchanged pleasantries in the usual manner, she said, "It's going to be a hot one out today."

Alfred then quickly replied "You always do look hot out on any day Mrs. Breaston."

She said, "Well, thank you Alfred, you aren't looking so bad yourself."

He always liked giving her or one of the other women on his floor a nice compliment every morning, he would say it to make them feel good about themselves, but somehow it always made him feel even better. He rushed to press the down button on the elevator as he always did.

They reached the ground floor and said goodbye as he called for a cab. "TechOne Software." He uttered to the driver as they sped away, "You know where that is don't you?"

"Of course you must be making the real money if you work there."

"The pay is not bad at all and I really like working there."

"Well that's good it sure must be better than driving this cab."

To make the poor cabbie feel better about himself Alfred says, "I bet driving people around New York everyday can be pretty exciting sometimes."

"Well, not exactly it gets pretty boring on most days."

"Well this is it, we're here, thanks for the ride see you again it was nice talking to you have a good day?" He got out of the cab and hurried in the main entrance thinking he could be a few minutes late. Just before he could sit down at his desk he noticed two men approaching him with a rather determined look on their faces.

"Are you Alfred von Monk?" One of the suits asked, as he searched the room to find some sort of explanation for their serious tone of voice.

"Yes, I am Alfred von Monk how can I help you two gentlemen today?"

The two men looked at each other and nodded their heads and one of them said, "Well, there is something that we need to talk to you about but we cant do it here you are going to have to come with us."

Alfred glanced at the serious look on both of their faces then said, "Now just wait a minute here I don't know who you are with but there is nothing that we cant talk about here at my desk." He hesitated for a second looked around at his desk and said, "Well I guess we could use one of the conference rooms I am sure that his early in the morning that there is one of them available."

The man, still wearing his sunglasses, put his finger to his ear as if he was listening to something, moved his head, then replied "No, I think that you will have to come with us there is something urgent that we need to talk about."

Somehow he knew that they weren't with the Microtech project and that they did not want to discuss software. "Before I go anywhere with you guys you are just going to have to tell me exactly who you are."

"I am agent Magnum"

The other suit says, "I am agent Morgan we are with the FBI."

Alfred takes a deep breath and scratches his forehead as sweat starts poring down and says, "The FBI what the heck is this some kind of joke? I have written no software codes that have ever come close to breaking any type of copyright infringement laws, so you guys better have a good reason to come into my office and ask me to leave like this, I have work that has to be finished by next week and I am already behind schedule so what is this all about?"

Agent Magnum looks at agent Morgan shakes his head and has a quick laugh before they get down to business thinking the copyright law worries was pretty funny, then says, "Well Alfred, I wish that it was only software that was the nature of our business that we are here today however, there has been an incident that demands your immediate presence at our offices."

He immediately goes to put back on his coat and says, "Well then I guess if I can be of any help to you then sure I will go with you."

As Alfred and the agents were leaving the TechOne tower several of his co-workers were giving him a smug expression as Ewing blurted out, "What did you do to get in trouble this time Alfred."

Agent Magnum then inserted, "Don't worry guys I am sure we will have him back in no time."

Ewing was a tall guy that all of Alfred's co-workers used to joke about while at the water cooler they used to say that he looked like the missing link, of course they would never tell Ewing that he could probably beat all of them up very easily. Agent Morgan then turned to Alfred and said, "Yeah, this wont take long at all we just need to ask you a few questions and then we will let you get back to work."

Alfred said, "Anything that I can do to help."

Once they reached the FBI registered car he noticed that the agents weren't talking that much and they were continually putting their finger up to their ear listening to something that Alfred could not hear. On the way to the local FBI office Alfred just sat in the back seat admiring the scenery of all the tall buildings wondering what all of this was about.

As they arrived at the FBI office agent Magnum started beeping as he fumbled around his suit coat trying to find his cell phone he finally answered it and with a rather serious tone, "I understand we are on our way now, yes he is with us, no, no problems or resistance everything is under control we will be there in a second."

Brainstorming the conversation trying to figure out what the guy on the other end was saying Alfred was thinking that his presence there better not be that important that would require a conversation like that. They reached the ground floor up from the parking lot and embarked on entering in the main entrance with rows of metal detectors that lead to another set of elevators.

Alfred emptied all of his pockets and put all of his belongings into a plastic container held by another agent with sunglasses on and all. He forcefully walked through looking over both of the walls of the detector thinking that it better not beep.

Sure enough it did and he had to go back through as Magnum asked, "You are not carrying any weapons are you?"

Alfred startled at the accusation interjected, "I work at TechOne now why would I even own any weapons?"

Magnum replied, "We never know what kind of psychos that we interrogate."

Dancing in Alfred's head he envisioned all of the movies that saw about the FBI trading bullets with some crazy psycho and understood the precaution. Alfred added, "I totally understand the precautions that must be taken into consideration when interacting with a possible criminal, but no, I don't even own a weapon so you don't have to worry about that it was just my cell phone that I forgot to take out of my suit, here watch it won't beep this time."

And just as Alfred said he walked right on through with no beeps and he recollected all of his belongings and headed for the elevators following the agents. There was a TV in the elevator that they all monitored as they ascended to their floor. He couldn't hear the audio all that well as a few of the other agents, going to a different floor, were in a heated discussion about something that he knew nothing about.

In the fleeting minute that they were on the elevator he noticed that there were news cameras with reporters outside of the Afghanistan Capitol but couldn't quite make out with what they were saying with the other agents making so much noise. They exited at the designated floor and were met with gray walls and inserted white doors as a suit exited one and went in another as they arrived at a door on the left side and entered into a very intimidating room. The walls were freshly painted with a gray hue and in the center of the room was a large gray table with chairs all around it.

Sitting back in a chair Alfred noticed a very large mirror on the far wall of the room, he knew what this was for he had seen it in many a movie but he couldn't believe that he was actually in this situation. Agent Magnum and Agent Morgan both simultaneously sat down in the chairs on each side of him. Agent Magnum interjected the silence with an abrupt, "Ok Alfred, you need to know that the whole following conversation is being recorded with audio and video devices behind that mirror so we need full cooperation from you and please do not leave out any detail in anything that we ask."

Alfred agreeingly answered, "I will do the best that I can to answer any of your questions."

Alfred was still conducting a quick brainstorm of all of the programs and contracts that he was involved with in the past year that he was with Tech One and couldn't think of anything that would explain the situation that he was in now. Starring at his reflection in the mirror he was thinking how good he would look if all of this were on TV or in a movie. The agents were both combing through their papers from their briefcase obviously looking for some important document to begin the questioning as Alfred blurts out from the frantic silence, "Is there any chance of this conversation being on some reality show on TV, you know that that would be really cool if it were, you guys should of called me this morning and I would have really dressed up for this role."

Agent Magnum then quickly interrupted, "Now you listen to me Alfred von Monk what we are about to discuss is very serious and if you are not going to take this seriously then we will get Brutus in here to rough you up and then see if you will take this seriously."

Alfred abruptly shook his head and uttered with a shaking jaw, "You can't really do that can you?"

"Just watch us."

"Ok, ok enough with the jokes I get the idea."

Agent Magnum shuffled his papers again and put one in front of the others and began the questioning, "Ok, here we go, Alfred how well do you know Angelica Perry?"

"Well I don't know her at all, Christie Columbo would speak of her every now and then when we were on the internet or on the phone other than that I don't know her at all, we have never met."

Morgan interjected his comments with, "Okay, so you are telling us that you know of her but you have never met her is that correct?"

Alfred responded, "Yes, that's right I know of her but we have never met."

Going through his papers agent Magnum goes, "The FBI has had a surveillance team on her for the past month and we are investigating a possible connection of her business the Traccia Italian Food chain with the Italian mafia, of which she is using Traccia's as a means of laundering money from the Italian mafia and she is not reporting it on her taxes. We now have enough evidence to convict her of tax evasion. Has Christie ever told you about any of this?"

Alfred was looking quite puzzled, "No she has never mentioned any of this at all. What does any of this have to do with me?"

"Okay, we will get to that in just a minute, a week ago on Wednesday night we were tapping her phone calls and overheard a conversation with Angelica and Christie Columbo. They talked for over an hour and had some really good things to say about you well, Christie did and I take it that you don't know Angelica."

Alfred goes, "Okay so what did she have to say about me?"

"Well, most of the conversation was about you and your meeting earlier that day, we can tell that she thinks very highly of you, however there was one thing that she said that was brought to our attention that created a security risk. During the course of the conversation Christie brought up the subject of her trip the next day to London where the corporate headquarters of Futura is located and said that she had asked you which plane to take and that you told her to use Continental and that it was the plane that you always took when flying to England. So what we are asking is did you or did you not tell her which plane to take?"

Alfred searched for something to say, "Yes, I remember the conversation, and yes, I did tell her to take the Continental plane. Okay you brought me all the way to these offices to ask me this? Can I go now?"

Alfred got up from his seat and headed for the door. "Not so fast there Monk we're not through with you yet, have a seat, we still have a lot more questions that have to answer."

Obviously frustrated he slammed the legs of the chair on the floor as he took his seat and muttered something that the agents couldn't hear, probably a cuss word. Calming down he took a deep breath and leaned back in his chair and says mockingly, "Okay, let's just answer those questions."

Agent Magnum looks around and shakes his head, "So tell us Monk, have you heard from Christie since your meeting with her a week ago?"

"No, not a call or an email I haven't heard from her at all."

"Do you know why you haven't heard from her?"

Getting very mad at the question he says, "No I don't know, I have no idea, maybe it was something that I said but I can't think of any reason that she would not keep in contact like this for almost a week. And I suppose you can tell me why she hasn't called. You are the FBI ya'll are supposed to know everything about anyone."

Agent Magnum was thinking that obviously he is just messing with us trying to get us to tell him what he already knows has happened. "Very good Monk playing dumb, listen here you better tell us everything that you know or it could get rough in here if you know what I mean."

Alfred was envisioning what it would be like if he really did get in a fight with these guys, he was sure he could take them, well if they didn't have guns. "I told you everything that I know, now you better tell me everything that you know."

"Okay, if that is how it is going to be. Tell us Alfred do you ever watch the news?"

"No, I never watch the news I can't stand it why do you ask?"

"Christie Columbo is dead, Alfred."

"What? What are you talking about, she isn't dead she just hasn't called that's all."

"The flight that you told her to get on crashed that next morning, she is dead along with every other passenger on the plane, they are all dead. Now why would you tell her to get on a plane that you knew was going to crash?"

Alfred takes a sigh of relief and kind of smiles, "Is this all some kind of joke or something, is all of this on TV? I am sure it is, TV's Bloop's Blunder's and Practical Jokes I have seen the show before, okay, everyone can come out now this is not very funny."

"Alfred von Monk you are accused of conspiring to conduct terrorist activity. Do you have anything to say for yourself?"

Alfred wondered what was going on with the sergeant as he began his questioning. He had never been accused of anything in his life so why would the sergeant begin this type of questioning now what had happened that would make the sergeant accuse him of murder. There had to be some logic behind his madness for him to actually accuse him of this. But what has this logic Alfred wondered who had he killed that they were accusing him of, what was going on. Why was the police questioning him about a murder. He could not figure it out he had never meant any harm to anyone in his whole life so why was the police questioning him about a murder. There had to be some logic behind this madness.

Chapter 6

THE INTERROGATOR

As Lawrence Dykeheed entered the room he noticed that Alfred was calm as can be, he obviously was not worried about anything and he had a stature that was very calm and conducive to someone that had no cares in the world. Sargent Lawrence Dykeheed entered the room obviously for an interrogation he noticed that Alfred Von Monk was as calm as can be. "So can you tell me how you met Christie Columbo?" He handed Alfred Von Monk his business card as a mere formality?

"Well it all began as a conversation that was over the internet." As Alfred leaned forward with his arms resting on the table that was before him, he noticed that Lawrence was not wearing an actual Police uniform and he was in normal clothes well as normal as a Sergeant could dress. Lawrence was a very pudgedly fellow that was kind of short and probably liked eating a whole box of doughnuts before his cup of coffee in the morning.

Although the laughable demeanor that appeared before Alfred he somehow knew that pudgy jokes would not get him out of these outrageous accusations. Alfred wondered why he was in this position and why the Sergeant was interrogating him. What had he done that would warrant such an attempt at an actual interrogation. Lawrence then leaned forward towards Alfred and handed him his business card. As Alfred read his business card he had a humorous thought that resulted in him actually speaking his actual name.

"I will do all of the questioning around here from now on and you will answer the questions as I ask them. Alfred was then wondering what he was doing at an actual Police Station and how they had brought him before an interrogator that was asking him these weird questions. He had done nothing that was against the law and he knew it. So he was thinking that all of this was just some kind of joke that his friend was playing on him and that this would result in some kind of prank. Well Lawrence Dykeheed had other thoughts as Alfred soon found out.

His questions began with "what is your relationship with Christie Columbo?"

Alfred then responded some what hesitantly with a reply as such" I know Christie as a friend that I met on the internet."

"So what can you tell me about her disappearance?" as Sergeant Dykeheed offered Alfred a cigarette and Alfred graciously accepted. He then lit his cigarette with the lighter that Lawrence offered him.

He began to smoke it and asked "What are you talking about?" to the impulsive Lawrence Dykeheed.

Lawrence then said, "You know exactly what I am talking about don't try and play dumb with me Alfred I know exactly what happened and I have the tape to prove it."

Alfred then responded, "What are you talking about I met her on the internet and that is all that happened."

Lawrence said, " So can you explain what her answering machine says."

Alfred then asked "What are you talking about?" Lawrence took another drag of the almost finished cigarette.

Lawrence then demanded that, "You know exactly what I am talking about so just tell me how you met Christie!"

The television was on and Alfred did not have the nerve to turn it off at the present situation. Alfred was more worried about how that anyone would respond to his posting of this biography on matchmate.com. What he posted could be explained in only a few sentences. Well he was obviously desperate for an actual response to his posting of his biography and he did not over exaggerate his actual state of well being at the present time. He was very candid and he did not leave out the desperate part of his current situation.

His profile was as such "I am currently single and I have never been married and I am seeking a soulmate that has time to seek out my present situation and accept me for who I am. I am 6"1' and I weigh 200 pounds and I have an outgoing personality that is fun to be around with any type of company. I am an easy going person that is easy to get along with any type of personality so if you are interested then just send me an email or an Instant message and I will respond as soon as possible."

Alfred then looked at Lawrence the Sergeant and expected a look of unbelievability then he lowered his head and said that "We were just friends on the internet, really that is all of our relationship."

Back in the interrogation room at NYPD Lawrence the Sargent was thinking that this was too much information to take into consideration at this present time and he then motioned to the observers behind the mirrored glass that he would like to take a break from the proceedings of the interrogation with Alfred. So then he offered Alfred a cigarette from his shirt pocket and Alfred hesitated for a second and then decided that he would like to smoke one to cut all of the tension in the air of the room. Lawrence then handed him a cigarette and then began to leave the room to where Alfred did not know perhaps to speak with the detectives that were watching everything behind the mirrored glass.

The door was shut and he was alone in the room and lit the cigarette and was smoking it very quickly and he did not have an ash tray and flicked the ashes on the floor. Alfred was however, very eager to pour his heart out to the man that was so intentionally accusing him of this heinous crime that he felt that if only Lawrence could see his point of view from the situation that he would be released and the questioning would end and he could get back to work at TechOne and try to go over what the FBI agents had just told him. He never, for one second, thought that she was actually dead and was killed in a plane explosion as the agents had told him. He did however take this as a possibility due to the fact that he had not watched the news on TV in years. Alfred was smarter than the average bear and he had a unique philosophy on life and in all of his surroundings.

He was anything but shallow to the fictional representations that were the basis of all news shows on TV. He felt that if only that he could talk to Angelica that he would find out what really happened to Christie that would explain all of this. He knew that Angelica knew Christie more than anyone and that she would know what had really happened. He then decided that his one call today would be to Angelica and then he would find out if what the agents were telling him really had happened. He knew that he could not believe what was taking place on the news was reality.

He then finished his cigarette and put it out on the floor and then stomped on it to make sure it was out. He normally did not smoke cigarettes but this was an exception and he thought that by smoking it that it would relieve the stress that he had built up in telling Lawrence about his meeting with Christie. He knew what the FBI agents had accused him of and he knew that he should tell the Sargent everything that happened the night that they actually met in person at Traccia's restaurant.

After a taxi there the walked Christie to her apartment, after dinner at Traccia's, he felt very good about the potential future between himself and Christie and he knew that something was going on. Perhaps, he had said something that had offended her of which he could not pinpoint exactly what it was that made her not call him after that night but he knew that if anyone knew that really happened it would be Angelica. She would inform him of the actual events that took place in the following week.

However, he had never even been to a police station and he did not know of the actual proceedings and processes that would allow him to make his phone call to Angelica. He had seen the situation in so may movies of how all individuals that were accused of a crime were allowed to make one phone call a day to whomever that they so desired. So he thought that he was definitely awarded one phone call during his stay at the police station. He just didn't want to be locked up in a cell which he had seen in so many TV shows and movies an it looked absolutely awful.

Somehow he thought that if he were to tell the Sargent everything that had happened that Wednesday night with Christie that Lawrence would grant him a ticket out of the dreaded police station. From watching NYPD Blue he felt that he knew enough about the proper code of ethics that he could find a way out of this awful situation that he was in. He only hoped that this was not one of the situations where the accused criminal would have to stay for some duration in time in a cell in the police station.

Just then Lawrence then entered the room with a rather perplexed look on his face as if he was determined to keep him as long as they wanted. "So Alfred would you like another cigarette?"

Alfred was still buzzing from the other cigarette that he had just smoked and, "No thanks I am fine." The Sargent then took his seat across from him and shuffled through his notes that were obviously written by one of the detectives that were watching everything behind the mirrored glass as he put the stack papers ever so close to his eyes to see if he could decipher what they had written.

Lawrence then restarted the interrogation, "So can you begin where we had just left off?"

Alfred attempted to remember exactly where they were in the conversation before he left the room. "Sure I think that I was telling you about the phone conversation between Christie and I and we were about to hang up and go to sleep. I must ask you this before we continue, I know that I am entitled to at least one phone call and I would like to make that phone call right now." Lawrence was expecting to get right back into the conversation but he then knew that Alfred should be allowed one phone call and that they could pick up where they left off after he made the phone call.

"Yes, that would be fine do you need a phone book or do you know the number of the person that you would like to call?"

Alfred was not sure of the exact phone number where he could reach Angelica so he, "Yes, I will need a phone book to make sure that I have the right number."

Lawrence then responded, "Well then... if you will make your way with me out the door and follow me to the phone I will get you a phone book."

The Sargent stood up and opened the door for Alfred as they both left the room. After all of the talking that he had just done he had lost his sense of direction of exactly where he was in the police station and followed Lawrence around the corner to where the phone was hanging on the wall next to a closed door which was perhaps another interrogation room he thought.

Lawrence then entered another room across the hall went in and came out with a New York phone book in his hand. He then handed it to Alfred and said, "You only get one call today so call whoever you have to."

Alfred then anxiously flipped the pages of the phone book searching for Traccia's. It took him a while to actually get to the page that it was on but none the less he found it and proceeded to dial the number hoping that she was there at this time of day.

It was ringing on the other end then someone in a very distinct accent answered the phone, "Yello! How can I helpa you."

Alfred was glad that someone actually answered the phone and said, "Is this Traccia's Italian restaurant?"

The heavy accent on the other end answered, "Yup this is Traccia's would you likea to place an order?"

Alfred responded, "No, I would like to speak with Angelica Mason please."

The Traccia's employee then said, "I am sorry but you have justa missed her she was just here but I think that she left already, you know how she is and all always coming and going it is hard to keep track of such a busy woman."

Alfred was perplexed, "You don't understand I have to speak with her and right now so could you please go check to see if somehow she is still there?"

The voice then said, "I am sorry man but I justa saw her leave man you justa missed her, why dont I geta your number and she cana call you back after she returns does that sounda ok with you?"

Alfred was worried and had reason to be, "No, I don't think that you understand I have to speak with her and I mean right now she cant call me back because I am detained right now and I am only allowed one phone call. I am a good friend of Christie Columbo do you know who she is?"

The italian accent replied, "Yesa of course I know who Christie is she comesa in here all the timea she is Angelica's best friend but that does not make any difference Algelica isnt here righta now, but any friend of Christie's is a frienda of mine. So just tell me whata is going on and I will do my best to help you out until she getsa back."

Alfred was considering the possibility that this guy could tell Angelica what is going on and there might be a chance that she could bail him out if he needed it. "I dont have enough time to tell you everything that has just happened but I will tell you this. The NYPD is accusing me of murdering Christie Columbo and they are threatening to keep me locked up until they find out what happened to her. So if there is any way that Angelica could bail me out I would be eternally grateful to her and you."

The voice then said, "Listen I am so sorry for what has just happened to you, my name is Tony, I am Angelica's brother and I am good friends with Christie so what ever you need I will help you get out of the police station. Anything I can do to help out one of Angelica's friends. You justa stay there and when Angelica gets backa I will tell her everything that has happened and thena I will go and bail you outa, so how does thata sound?"

Alfred was relieved in a way, "Thank you so much Tony, Tell Angelica everything that is going on and when she gets back come and get me out of here ok?"

Tony said, "Sure thing there Alfred we will get you out of there in no time, I'll see you when I get there." Alfred then said, "Thanks again I will be looking forward to seeing you, goodbye."

Alfred then hung up the phone and followed the Sargent back to the interrogation room wondering how long it would take for them to get there. He sat down in his chair and gave an unpleasant stare into the mirrored glass, pissed at the people behind it for making him stay there so long. Lawrence began, "So where were we?"

Alfred said, "I was just telling you about the phone conversation on the week before we met." The Sargent then replied, "Sure go ahead," Alfred took a deep breath and...

Back in the interrogation room at NYPD Lawrence the sergeant was thinking that this was too much information to take into consideration at this present time and he then motioned to the observers behind the mirrored glass that he would like to take a break from the proceedings of the interrogation with Alfred. So then he offered Alfred a cigarette from his shirt pocket and Alfred hesitated for a second and then decided that he would like to smoke one to cut all of the tension in the air of the room. Lawrence then handed him a cigarette and then began to leave the room to where Alfred did not know. Perhaps to speak with the detectives that were watching everything behind the mirrored glass.

The Sargent was back and ready to hear what he had to say, "Can we do this again?"

Alfred was able to capture the exact emotions that he had whenever he finished the conversation with Christie and this was a feat that he had not accomplished in the previous encounters with his conversation with Lawrence. So he then began his journey into the unknown well at least to Lawrence and he then began to feel so comfortable with him that he was wanting to capture the specific emotions that would elaborate upon in this revealing conversation.

His moment in time that he shared with her when they were on the phone was very terse but ever so inspirational and he felt a desperate need to rethink this short but ever so meaningful conversation with this incredible woman that had so enthusiastically imbued his life for this short period of time that to him felt like an eternity. He could live forever in the moment that he had shared with this inspirational woman. Words alone could never describe the emotions that were streaming through his brittle heart throughout the course of the fateful night that he had just experienced with her.

How could words alone ever capture all of the juxtaposed emotions that he was feeling at the exact moment that he hung up with Christie this was an impossible feat that Tom Cruise couldn't even accomplish in any of his movies. This was the exact theme that was running through his head after he hung up with her he so desperately wanted to pour out all of his love struck emotions that he was feeling at the time and this was definitely a Mission Impossible. He somehow wanted to capture all of the essence of all of his traveling emotions that he was going through and he felt that he could best do this through writing his feelings down on paper. So that in the next night when they finally did actually did get to speak on the phone that he would have all of the perfect words to say to her that would make her feel absolutely incredible about the potential relationship that he saw forming between themselves.

In the conversation that they had just been apart of on the instant messenger as well as the intimate encounter on the phone he knew that this had the makings of a relationship that could last for eternity. Somehow he felt that God had given him the words to say to her both on the instant messenger as well as on the phone that had made him feel like that he was unstoppable in his epic adventure to find the perfect woman and he thought that in every way that he had finally found his potential and more of a realistic potential to find his soul-mate. He had never felt this way so soon about any woman even the possible love of his uneventful life with his previous love in Lisa.

How could this be that in the brief encounter with this angel of an absolute stranger was he able to revel his exact extrapolation of his precise emotions and feelings to this incredible woman. He then thought to himself that she was perfection in the making. For the short while that they had exchanged ideas and emotions he felt that this was an event that would affect the rest of his soon to be ever so meaningful life. Up until this point he had had the faint premonition that it was realistically impossible to ever find an infinite soulmate again.

For so long he had mourned the breakup between himself and Lisa that he was not able to fathom the possibility of ever finding this sort of love in his life ever again. However when he finally hung up the phone tonight with Christie he had a distinct feeling that was so overwhelming in all of his fragile senses that this was the potential woman that he was meant to be with for the rest of his life. This was a historic kind of love that writers and poets attempted so desperately to capture in verse that he was somehow experiencing in real life.

Was this actually possible he thought to himself his innermost instincts told him that this was indeed the case and he should reflect on this experience with the utmost of respect and admiration for what he felt was the beginning of an epic relationship that any human had ever dreamed of having throughout the entire course of human history. He only prayed that Christie herself was having the exact same feelings that he was having at this exact moment. With a potential so ever profound in his heart of hearts he could only dream that she was somehow was thinking the exact same thing that he was feeling at this intimate sort of reflection after such an eventful sort of conversation. Could this actually be the fate that he had only seen in the most realistic of movies.

One of his favorite and most cherished movies that he held so dear to his heart was the epic love of Noah and Allie that was portrayed in the movie the notebook. This movie was able to capture the very essence of everything that people should dream that love should be. The simple love of one man for another woman had inspired him to dream even bigger than he ever thought he was capable of. This love this profound exchange of raw emotions that was seen in this movie was everything that he dreamed that love should be like in reality. He thought so intently of how they met and how fate had stepped in and taken control of the very fiber of their being, and somehow he felt that someday when he and Christie had grown old together and had experienced life and love to the fullest that someone would actually write of their relationship just as they did with Noah and Ali.

Some could call him a passionate dreamer or a man who now lived with his head in heaven. Somehow this conversation had given him a vision of what love should really be like when people actually find their soul-mate. He thought for a while and was covered in reflection as he glanced though his relationship with Lisa and he came to the realization that he had never felt this way with her. Was this the void that was missing in his relationship with her that prevented them from an infinite love that he was now feeling for this utter stranger. However he did not at all feel that his woman was a stranger in the least this was a woman that he knew that he could be with for the rest of his life. He knew that tonight was fate stepping into his life and he would be captured by the moment in what felt like an eternity.

How could such strangers find this in such an unexpected sort of meeting what they shared tonight could last for an eternity. He then decided that he would leave his infinite fate up to the heavens that would bless him with a dream that would be with him from the moment on. He only prayed that the potential blessing of a dream would inspire him with the perfect words that he would speak to Christie in the following night. Oh how he longed for the spiritual righteousness that would grant him a vision of what he should say to her tomorrow night. Fate was in the air and it encircled his mind as he slowly fell asleep reflecting on the inspiration that he had just known in this amazing woman.

Lawrence was quite undertaken by this juxtaposed position of understanding the nature of the somewhat unconventional relationship that had developed the night of their actual conversation. He was not the kind of man that had ever experienced this type of love so early in the relationship and he felt that this was something that could never actually happen in his NYPD blue sense of the world. All he wanted was the good stuff or actually the good stuff that actually pertained to his perception of what would actually break the case in this awkward situation that he had haphazardly found himself immersing into.

He was continually reviewing all of the data that Alfred was so apt to delivering into something that his boss could actually find useful in the case that he had just found himself in. Alfred's words not only spoke to his heart they also revealed his intimate thoughts of wanting to get to know this woman as much as he did. Lawrence was ever so compelled to want to get to know this incredible woman as much as Alfred had in the short time that he actually did get to spend with her. His vision was just as angelic as the vision that Alfred had had of her on the night that she spoke.

Chapter 7

TONY AND THE COSTUME

"Whata the heck don't you know that you cant carry plates like that you think that you are a magician when you are just a humble apprentice in training. Cant you ever get it right what is wrong with you."

Tony felt no remorse for the new recruit that he was coaching into the business, even though he wished that the guys would have shown him some kind of remorse when he was going through the same thing. It aint easy bein cheesy they would say all things considered when orchestrating a multi million dollar flow of snow in the city. They called him doorag when he was cook creative cullinary creations he could steam up every thing like red hots as they would call it when he would throw some red hot chili peppers on a supreme pizza pie. Every waiter in Traccia's had previously been a nighttime deliverer for their godfather Antonio before they could actually work at Traccia's.

Angelica would never hire new wait staff if they hadn't passed the laborious tests that godfather Antonio had passed upon them. Here whether they were new recruits that had to be put before the examining board of her godfather that was such a revered ghost in the business that had so much weight in the say of what got done that this new man was definitely feeling the mirage that was the Italian Mafia.

Alfonzo Benzanini was beyond the scope of reason when it came to entering a new arena of loyalty that he had just been introduced to. "Tony, I ama so sorry, tell me what I need to be doing and heya I am gonna do it for you, for the godfather anything heya I am here. Just say the words and I ama here."

Tony had run the restaurant side of the business for over a decade and he knew all of the various tactics of stressing out the new recruits on the day of their inception. "Alfonzo what area youa gonna do when you get some real customers, when the sun is shining in your facea? You have to know by now that we always receive some high status diplomats that eat here all of the time you have got to know the language before you enter into a meeting of a true man of diplomacy. I tella you what tonight after your shift I have got a mission for you."

Tony uttered all of the grueling details that preluded him and found him to be a true man of his word." Angelica burst through the front door without an introduction, but none the such was needed with her commanding presence as important as Tony was to the show Angelica had the presence of a real leader and nothing got done without her say in the matter.

"Tony, what you got cookin?" She asked, as she fervently made her way into the kitchen.

Tony aptly replied, "I gotta new friend in the business and Ia think that you justa might know this fellow."

Angelica was looking at the pasta that had to be a few minutes late in getting it to a demanding table and said, "So who is this new mystery man?"

Tony looking at the order of lasagna that was obviously overdue to be taken out by the new recruit and focused in on the discussion and said, "Do youa know a guy that came in here about a week ago that goes by the name of Alfred von Monk?"

Angelica picked up the lasagna and threw it into the hands of the recruit Alfonzo and jutted her hands toward the table that it was supposed to go to. "Sure, I know Alfred, he is a good friend of Christie's."

Tony in the managerial position said something to Alfonzo that hurried his approach to the table that was expecting the lasagna. "How much cheese you got on you sis?"

Angelica then pushed Alfonzo carrying the plates out the swinging doors ever so gently on the shoulder and gave words of inspiration that would send a smile rushing through the restaurant. "I've got enough to turn some heads whatcha need?"

Tony then followed the recruit through the maze of tables to the arrival of his awaited journey with his eyes through the window from the kitchen. "Alfred is in some serious beef with the blues and he needs our help."

Angelica eyeingly stalked the recruit as he gently placed the lasagna on the table of the awaiting couple that were ever so pleased with the food. "How soon?" She knew exactly what he was saying without any further words. She pieced together the info as she recalled the events of the past week. Tony knew his response was hanging in the wind when he said, "ASAP sister they have got him mixed up with tha gators."

Angelica stopped everything that she was doing and looked Tony in the eyes and said, "Lets go."

Tony put down the pizza that he was spinning and uttered the prophetic words, "Someday, someday we are really gonna be free." In a whirlwind they both breezed through the back door to a car that started with the punch of a button, somehow the sports car knew the ride that they were about to embark upon, after all Mercedes Benz were always ready for the adventure ahead. They were in the same general state of mind as they sped away to find what would be waiting for them. Angelica's phone was playing an old forgotten song as she fished it out of her left side pocket and answered with a terse hello. She was rambling on in her everso energetic tone of pulse.

All Tony heard was, "Chile you gotta add tha chile." She then withdrew her phone back into her pocket and set it for vibrate. Before they knew it they were immersed into a barrage of uniformed officers that were not expecting the arrival of a benz in their coveted parking spaces they parked there anyway. Their pace toward the elevators was filled with anticipation as they pressed their way toward the main floor from the parking garage.

They had seen the scene all too often with their cohorts falling prey to the stalking officers that just envied their freedom. Angelica spoke up as they glanced at the two globes of lights in their hasty arrival. "We are here for Alfred von Monk how much is the bail?"

Angelica fished her wallet out of her purse with feathers and all that was laced with fur and gazed upon the cash that she had yet to deposit in the neighborhood bank. The lady at the front desk then rummaged through the papers that were stacked upon her cluttered desk and said, "Could you wait a moment while I retrieve the info?"

After a few minutes it was obvious that she couldn't find any paperwork that pertained to Alfred and she then began to strike her computer in the attempt to find anything on this mystery man. A smile came over her face as she stammer across the right info that detailed the stay of Alfred in the interrogation room. She jotted down some notes in her notebook as she scrolled through Alfred's info. When she reached the end of the text she began to ask who these individuals were. Angelica said that they were good friends and wanted to know how much it was going to be to bail him out.

The lady at the desk said, "$9,000," as a man in the lemming uniform approached her and whispered something into her ear. Angelica then started counting her dough and realized that she needed to reach the ATM located just around the corner. After she retrieved the money from the ATM she made her way back to a long line of people from all different walks of life as Tony motioned her to the front of the line.

She counted out the money to the police clerk placing each bill on top of the other, "There $9,000 present and accounted for."

The man that had been whispering into her ear was still standing there and said, "I am sorry ma'am there seems to be a glitch in the system von Monk is no longer able to be released with bail."

Tony got this look on his face like everything was kosher such serenity had not been seen on his mug in such a long time. "Oh, I see thanks for your help there good looking." Within a microcosm he glimmered an intriguing idea that caught his notion as only he could say it "I have a plan".

The look in his eye was sentimentally unpronounceable it was as if his high school sweetheart had just said yes to the very question that he never had the courage to ask. Angelica had seen this light in his eye only on a very rare or monumental occasion.

Minutes bounced by as the eye of the tiger got a gleam in Tony's eyes as he sifted through the sea of people bumping and pushing through the crowd. He pounced on this new idea and nothing was going to get in his way as the tall Italian Mafia man's presence parted the sea finally reaching the destination, "Bloomington's Costumes."

His brown, slick as chrome, alligator loafers clanked on the antique wooden floor making his way to the counter cluttered with postcards and knick nacks from all over the world. He brushed them by with the elbow of his Italian pin striped suit. There was a homely looking woman that had no clue that in this century women wear makeup. He expected her Omish husband Jedakiah to come dancing around the corner any minute. "Hey you gota some gooda costumes do ya?"

Confident in her meek ways she humbly said, "Yes sir we have everything what do you need?"

Angelica was right behind him and following him every step of the way. She nudged him in the back as he spoke up, "Yo! I'd like a nice NYPD uniform. You got it?"

"Let me go and see." She ducked behind the curtain to where all of the clothes were Tony thought she better hurry it up. "She better likea maka move on it. There is no telling what they are doing to poor Alfie."

"He'll be fine."

"You never know, I sawa this show on TV where these police detectives were interrogating this poor chap and they got out this thing that you see at the dentist's office and cut out part of his tongue. I don't want nothin happenin to our Alfie. Ya know?"

"He'll be fine, and if they rough him up we'll sick Gonzo on them."

"Oh, I like that. Gozo would make those police types quiver in their boots."

The Ahmish lady springs back from behind the curtain with a suit in her draped over her arm and says, "See if this one fits." She held it out in front of her.

"Lady my sister Angelica couldn't wear that thing. I'm a pretty big guy you got anything in an extra large?"

"Wait a minute I'll be back."

She shakes her head and disappears again. Tony looked over to Angelica and said, "Goodness I'm no freakin midget."

"It's little people Tony, look there's one now." Tony tips his Tom Landry hat to the little person and says, "Sorry there guy I didn't know they were calling midgets little people now. Next thing you know they'll make me say vertically challenged."

"It's no problem sir, I am just looking for a costume here."

"If you want they have this police uniform that might be your size."

The little person didn't say anything and Angelica nudged Tony in the back. "Tony...goodness you have to learn to be nicer than that."

"Those guys are funny looking. Hey, did I make you laugh?"

"Okay, yeah I guess it was kind of funny."

The owner lady popped out with yet another uniform. "This is the biggest that we have. Oh yeah, this one is refurbished."

"Refurbished? My laptop is refurbished, what did you do? How does it look?"

"It looks fine I just had to sew it up on the collar, see good as new. Back in business?"

"Yeah it'll do."

"The dressing room is over there."

"Thanks lady, Ia really appreciate this." He grabbed the NYPD blue uniform and headed straight for a curtain room on the side of the store. After a few minutes of trying it on he says, "Angelia, wait till you getta load of this."

"How is it?"

"It's perfect, man this thing is great."

"Let get going now Tony we don't have all day here."

With his suit in hand he asks the store lady, "How much is it?"

"$100.00 per day."

"I only need it for a few hours. Okay I'll take it."

They were out the door with his clothes in a bag that Angelica was carrying as they sifted through the New York crowd. Tony was looking as sharp as ever in his new uniform he really looked legit and like someone that you didn't want to mess with. They made it to the station just about out of breath, the uniform was pretty hot being wool and all for Tony. Angelica stayed outside and waited for them to emerge as Tony walked right through the front entrance and into the back rooms.

He had to find the interrogation room that Alfie was in so Tony did his best to remember what Alfie had said. An officer noticed that Tony looked a little out of place so he asked him, "Looking for someone?"

"Yeah, as a matter of fact I am, Sargent Dykeheed. You know him?"

"Sure do. He's in the middle of an interrogation right now, can it wait?"

Tony confidently said, "No, it can't wait. This is about Monk I'm here to take him back to the CIA."

"Right this way sir."

"Thank you."

The officer opened the door to the room and Tony introduced himself. "Andy Sipowicz here. I need to take Monk over to the CIA for some questioning."

Sargent Dykheed stood up and said, "I haven't heard anything about this. Do you have any papers?"

"Listen they are waiting for him at the headquarters are you gonna make me call my boss so you can talk to him."

"That won't be necessary. He's yours."

"I'll take him from here, I appreciate it men."

"No problem."

Tony and Monk were quietly leaving the room as Tony took him by his bicep and roughly shoved him out the door. "We gotta talk to you punk!" Alfred looked at him funny.

As soon as they saw Angelica it was smiles all over. They swiftly paced their way to Angelica's car as Tony removed the handcuffs once they were in the car. They sped away leaving no trail as to what they had just done. Finally they could talk, Tony was first, "That was a close one back there Alfie, you alright?"

"Shaken up a little. Other than that I'm fine. I can't thank you guys enough."

"Don't mention it. A friend of Christie's is a friend of mine."

Chapter 8

LIFE'S GOOD

The upstairs apartment of Angelica was plush and quite luxurious, paid for by the Italian Mafia of course. Tony was in front of the mirror in the restroom and he was shaving with his new Monty electric shaver that gave a buzzing noise throughout the living room where Angelica and Alife were sitting down to talk. Her lush brown pillows on the couch were very comfortable and Alfie eased back into a desirable position with his elbow on the rest. Angelica was on the edge of a fine, ornate, silver and magenta tapestry chair.

Angelica was getting calls from all kinds of people and for the moment her phone was quiet so they began to talk. "There is something that I have to tell you about Christie."

"What is it?"

"You know we have been friends forever, well it seems that she is in continental..." She stopped in mid sentence, her phone vibrated in her top left pocket over her breast that couldn't be heard by Alfie.

"Well that's none of my business. One time when I was in school some of the guys thought it would be funny to slip my some ex-lax in my coffee."

She slipped the vibrating phone out from her pocket and answered it. Alfie fell silent as she began to talk. "Christie! Where are you?" He could slightly make out a discernible pattern in the tone of voice and knew that it must be Columbo. His heart leapt from his chest beating a thousand miles an hour. With all that was within him he wanted to be the one talking to her now instead of Angelica, but he would have to wait if he would even get the chance at all.

"That's horrible, at least you're okay...we can help, Tony and Gonzo and the guys would be more than happy to...just give me the address...well then when will I see you again?...run Christie run!"

"We have to get to her." Alfie said concerned and worried out of his mind.

"She said that she wants for you to go and get her laptop from her apartment, climb in the back window here is the address. Hurry up and go now and Tony and I will find out where she is and meet us back here. We won't leave without you."

"Okay, I'm gone." Alfie ran out the door and hopped the next bus to the address on the post-it note.

Angie called out, "Tony put down that shaver and get in here right now."

"Just a minute Angie."

"Tony!"

"Okay, okay." He came strolling in with part of his face shadowed with stubble. "What?"

"It's Christie, she is in trouble."

"She's alive?"

"Yes and terrorists are after her. They might already have her by now. We have to hurry can you call Guido and see if he can get a trace on the last phone call from this phone? "

"Yeah, he'sa probably eating a Pizzone right about now. Let me call him."

Tony yelled into the phone like Guido was hard of hearing, "Guido! You there!"

"Yeah I'm here!" Guido yelled back. "Is this Tony?" He yelled again like some gangster mafia movies.

"Yeah this is Tony. Heya I'ma gonna need you to do a trace for me. Capishe?"

"Capishe, I'll be right over."

"Bring your stuff."

"What?" He yelled.

"Bring your stuff. You know the equipment for tracing." Tony yelled back at him.

"Okay. Chow."

"Poodle. Shit-zu, what are we naming our favorite dogs now or what?"

Tony was being a wise guy and Guido had already hung up the phone. They waited till they saw him pull up in the alley.

"Tony, hows yousa doin'?"

"Just great, now where's tha equipment knucklehead?"

"Its right here in this duffle bag." He plopped down the bag on the kitchen table and proceeded to take out just about everything in the bag.

"What did you bring your whole house in that thing?"

"Here it is."

"That's a cell phone?"

"Yeah, that's what I use to trace the calls Jerky. I've got this app that can trace anything."

"So what is all of this other stuff?"

"Oh that. Well, you said to bring the equipment so I brought everything." He started to pick objects up and tell what they did. "This will yank out the brain from the nose. This will pull out teeth."

"Okay, wea getta the idea. But hey, I meant phone tracing equipment there knucklehead."

"Oops."

"We need to find out where Christie is?"

"Columbo? That good looking girl that always wears those skirts. Great legs, goodness, what she in trouble?"

"Yeah and we need to find her."

"I'll tell you what, whoever has her we can use some of this equipment on them for taking Christie like that."

"Just do the trace."

"Okay, okay. Just a minute." Guido tapped out something on his phone, "Can I have your phone? The phone that received the call."

Angie said, "Sure thing."

"Alright." He typed in all the the info from Angie's phone and began the trace. "She's on the move right now, I gotta cell phone going fast down Broadway."

"Is there anyway to know if it is her?"

"We won't know unless we call her."

"We can't do that the terrorists will find out that she has the phone."

"Well, then I guess we will just have to chase her."

"We can do that in my benz." Music started coming from the phone in Guido's pocket, it was Angie's phone. He threw it towards her and she caught it and answered it immediately. "Hello."

"Angie, I've got the laptop and I'm on my way over."

"Don't bother, we'll come get you. Stay right there and see what you can find out about why Christie is in all this mess."

"Will do." The call ended and Alfie started clicking away on her laptop while Angie motioned for the guys.

"Let's go bozo's."

"Your car or mine Angie?" Tony asked.

"Let me think for a minute? You drive a 1968 Mustang and I have a new SLK. You know why mercedes calls it an SLK, See ya Later Kutie, its fast. We'll take the stang next time, okay?"

"Okay. Let's go." Tony said as he noticed Guido going in the opposite direction, Guido was putting all of the mid-evil equipment in the bag.

Guido looked at Tony and said, "Just in case."

"No you moron, we're not going to use any of that. Get your phone and let's go. We can use your phone. What kind is it an LG?"

"Yeah."

"Life's good now let's go Guido."

They ran out the door and down the stairs and out into the alley where Angie was revving up the engine to the SLK. They flew outta there like Jonas Salk to the bank, paper plates in their wake. Guido leaned forward from the back seat to listen to them talk.

"We get Alfie and then we find out where Christie is on Guido's phone."

"I found out it's an LG."

"That's great Tony, then we go to Christie and get her the heck outta there."

"Do you want for me to have Gonzo and the guys meet us there just in case there is any trouble?"

"Yes, Tony that would be fine."

Guido was listening to every word and following Christie on his new LG phone. Guido had something important to ask Angie you could tell by the intense look on his face. Maybe he had just figured out where they were taking Christie. "Do you know what LG stand's for Angie?"

"Let me guess..."

"That's a good one, actually it stands for Life's Good."

"That's great Guido. Have you found out anything new?"

"Nope, that's it."

"What's it?"

"Life's good."

"Oh goodness, yes Guido life is good. Let me know what you find out on Christie."

"Okay, Angie."

She raced down the streets and into an alley where Alfie was waiting. She stopped and he jumped in the back seat with the laptop clutched in his arms.

"What did you find out?"

"Oh goodness, life is so good..."

"Ya dont say."

"Listen up, did any of you guys know that Christie works for Futura and she was on her way to London to finish a project on a bomb?"

"What?"

"Well, missile really. Yeah she makes biological weapons people. She is a consultant to Global Defense the United States largest weapons contractor. That must be why those terrorists are after her."

"Finally someone is actually doing their homework here. Guido do you have anything on Christie."

"No, she's a great girl with great legs, devout Catholic, I could never have anything on her."

"No moron, your phone."

"Oh like that? Yeah she just went in the Waldorf Astoria."

"We're there." Angie punched it down the street in Union City, she knew exactly where she was going. Across the bridge they made it to New York the island of lights just south of Manhattan.

Alfie kept on going, "So this bomb that she was working on was just about to be put into production when the plane went down. She had been working for months on the compound and last month they tested the last batch in Arizona and it passed code specs. The chemical compound that made it to prototype was called Netrosia. Her folder on the research is called Rose of Death. There are also several documents called the rose."

"We're almost here. I'll park in the garage." They passed right in front of the Hotel and Guido noticed that there was a man out front selling roses by the sidewalk entrance.

"Good that's where I told the guys to meet us. The main entrance from the garage." Tony said, still on the phone with Gonzo.

She parked and they all got out and Tony slid his phone shut and put it in his shirt pocket. Angie reached in and got out her purse equipped with a 9 mm. glock and a taser for safe keeping. Alfie put the laptop in the trunk and shoved a pistol of his own down the back side of his jeans, leaving the butt sticking out. Guido pulled out his coat flap to show Alfie that he was packing heat. Showing his weapons holstered he said to Alfie, "Life'sa Gooda, hey?"

"Yeah, I would say so."

Tony was also a devout Italian Catholic and said, "God's good."

"That He is." Alfie agreed as he began to pace towards the entrance.

If anybody did mess with them they would be well armed to defend themselves no matter how terrible these terrorists were. On their way to the entrance they hear this thud that got louder and louder. It was music from a car, finally it was getting so loud that they could feel their weapons vibrate, but they still couldn't see the car. After a minute a Caddilac with six armed Italian brutes come sailing around the corner of the garage with Cypress Hill blairing some gansta rap song, Insane in the Membrane.

Tony recognizes Gonzo in the driver's seat and shout's over the music. "Heya Gonzo over here."

The car pulled up to Tony and Gonzo yelled, "What?"

"Turn down the music crazy."

"Insane in the Membrane, insane in the brain."

"Oh, the music, sure." The music is silenced as the window went further down. "Heya Tony, howsa it going?"

"Hurry it up."

"Okay we'll park."

In a minute they were all walking in the side garage entrance to the Waldorf Astoria. Alfie was looking for signs around the hotel as to where she might be. They had no idea what to look for or who to ask for at the front desk. The app on Guido's phone didn't give floor numbers it just had buildings and they were already there.

Alfie said to Angie, "How in the heck are we supposed to find her? There are 47 floors this could take forever."

"Ask Guido what his phone can do."

"I'll see if it can track altitude." Guido did his work and wasn't finding anything. "Wait...here it is. Altitude from sea level. It says 84 feet."

Alfie had made several software programs that could calculate this but all he had was his cell phone calculator. "Alright, tell me what our altitude is right now on this floor."

"Just a minute...alright it says 44 feet above sea level."

"Great, there are ten feet in a floor so that would make her position at the 4th floor."

Angie was impressed, "Let's go then guys, shesa waiting." She had been hanging around the Italian accented Tony so long that he was beginning to make an impression on her.

They all went to the elevators, Alfie pressed the 4 button it lit up and they were on their way without a clue of how to find her on the floor. It dinged and the 4th light was glowing and they all exited onto the plush carpet of the floor.

"I say we go to each door and ask for her."

"No one asked what you think we should do Guido."

Alfie had an idea, "I say we all just scout the area out and see if we can find any clues as to where she is, maybe listen to some doors and see if we hear her."

Angie agreed, "What are you morons waiting on? Let's go."

Angie and Alfie took a right along with Gonzo and Guido the rest of them went with Tony to the left. Angie noticed there were several dishes out on the floor in front of some of the rooms. Guido stuck his ear up to each door as the rest of them just walked on looking for something.

Alfie saw something, "Look there is a silk rose, just the bud, she must be close."

"Why? A rose it could be from anyone."

"Remember the name of the chemical compound of missile that she was working on was called Netrosia. The rose is it, this has to be where she is."

"If you think so Alfie." Angie said unenthusiasticly.

"She must have got the rose from the front of the building when the terrorists were taking her here."

Alfie knew he must be right. "I think you're right Guido. It must be this next room 410, I'll ring the buzzer." It rang and rang but no one answered. Alfie decided to look for some other rooms and when he leaned up against the door it swung open.

Much to his surprise Christie was sitting on a chair tied up in the center of the room. She had duck taped around her mouth and she was saying something that they couldn't understand with all the tape on her mouth. Angie went to go and get the rest of the guys in case there were any of the terrorists still around. Guido and Gonzo would stay and help Alfie and Christie. Alfie rushed over to her and began taking off the duck tape, being careful not to tear her hair out in the process.

When all of the tape was removed she screamed, "The door, don't let the door lock."

Guido was the last one through and it was already closing and it was pretty close to being shut. Alfie got scared that the bomb on her would go off if it closed and locked. He yelled, "Run, get it."

The closet blocked off the view from where Alfie and Christie were to see if the door had closed or not. A light went green on her chest, they thought that it surely must have closed.

Panicked all Christie could do was scream, "Ahhhh!"

Tony came busting in through the door before Guido could get there and the light went back to the off state. Tony had saved the day and there was no one happier in the room than Christie.

"Thank you God. Tony, God bless you."

Tony just went through he had no idea what he had just done, "Christie, I thought I would never see you again."

Alfie was concerned about her safety, "Now we just have to take this bomb off of you."

Her face was tensed and frantically she said, "No you can't. It is set up to that computer over there on the table. You have to disarm it first."

"Okay, just calm down we will figure this out."

Angie knew Alfie had experience in software, "Can you fix it Alfie?"

"Let me see what we have here."

Gonzo said, "I think we should call the cops."

"Let Alfie do this." Angelica said impatiently.

He went over to the table and sat at the chair and the laptop started a countdown...10...9...8. He had to do something fast. He grabbed the mouse and clicked on the screen and nothing it continued to countdown. 4...3...2. There was an icon on the screen so he clicked on it. A window opened up that said, "You have ten minutes to complete this test or Christie will die. Starting now. You must have a score of over 140 to pass.

"What is it Alfie?"

"I think it's some kind of I.Q. Test."

"Can you pass it?" Angie asked worried for her friend still trapped in the chair.

"I don't know."

Christie wished there was something she could do so she said, "Quick, everyone pray for Alfie."

Guido started out, "Father in the name of Jesus don't let the bomb go off, I have a wife and children."

Angie was preturbed, "Not out loud you knucklehead, you'll break his concentration."

"Oh, sorry."

Christie now noticed that it was Alfie that had come to her resuce and knew how intelligent that he was, "I know you can do it Alfie, just do your best."

"Thanks." He answered the first question that said, "What would you name this book." It had a picture of a man in the background and a woman bringing him some tea and it over looked a river or some body of water.

Multiple choice answers were: A. Adventures on the Rhine
                                    B. Getting to know you
                                    C. Sad day in Paradise
                                    D. Starting a business

He had never heard of this book and didn't know the right answer so he gave it his best shot and guessed...A. Adventures on the Rhine

Next question, apparently he wouldn't know what his score was until after the test was over.

Tony said, "Don't worry about it Alfie I think you got it right."
"Thanks."

The next question said, "The words triangle glove clock bicycle all correspond to these numbers 3,5,12,2. True or False

True

Next Question: 27 minutes before 9 o'clock is 33 minutes past 8 o'clock. True or False?

True

Gary has only 50$ and wants to buy a bicycle for 130, if he borrows 61 from Jane and 21 from Jill he has enough to buy the bicycle. True or False?

True

A round wall clock has been rotated upside down when it is at 2:45 the minute hand will be facing right. True or False?

True

The words education, cautioned, and auctioned all use the exact same letters. True or false?

True

9 chickens 2 dogs and 3 cats have 40 legs? True or False?

False.

If the thumb is a finger then 3 gloves and 3 shoes should hold 35 fingers and toes. True or False?

False

If Monday is the first day of the month then the next Thursday is the fourth day of the month. True or False

True

Three of the following numbers add up to 33. 17,2,3,19,6
True or False?

False

He was finally done with the test and now they were ready to find out what his score was. They all prayed silently that he would pass, if not they were all toast. Tony didn't want to wait around and see so he and all of the guys took off running down the hall to the elevator. Not that they didn't think that Alfie could pass it but they just wanted to be sure, no reason for all of them to die.

Angie stayed with them and finally the computer gave the results...

You have scored 141 and have passed the test. We will come looking for her, beware.

Christie was so happy and thankful that a huge smile overcame her with a tear in her eye she said, "Thank you Alfie, Thank God for you. Now get me outta this thing."

Alfie went over to her and took the bomb vest off and gave her a huge hug or rather she gave him the hug accompanied by a big kiss on the lips.

"What you did was heroic, thank you so much."

"It was nothing ma'am just doing my part to help a good friend." Alfie said in his best John Wayne accent. She laughed and they held hands as they went out the room and into the hall. Angie followed as they made it to the elevator and found that the guys must be down stairs already. They weren't in the lobby and Angie got worried so she called Tony.

"Hey Tony!"

"Yo, Angie. We got some problems ova heer."

"What kinda problems Tony?"

"Terrorists."

"We'll be there in a minute."

Alfie, Angie and Christie all rushed from the lobby out to the garage to find Tony and the guys shooting it out with the terrorists. They pulled out their guns and Angie ran over to Tony and they knelt behind a BMW and she asked, "What happened?"

"Gonzo and I were going out to our cars and he noticed someone messing with his car. They had broken in and was messing with the stereo.

Gonzo started shooting at them then this van came by and shot at all of us with these Afghan machine guns. We just ducked behind these cars and no one got hit. They drove over to that pylon and they have been firing at us ever since."

Gonzo was really getting pissed so he shot his last round at the driver of the van. The shooting stopped then they got a new driver and drove away. That's when things got interesting.

"Heya Tony, what do you think they did to my car?"

"I don't know. Go start it up and see."

"I'm not starting it. What if they rigged some kinda bomb to it or somfin?"

"Let me have the keys. I'll start it."

Gonzo threw him the keys and Tony walked over to the car and looked underneath it and saw absolutely nothing. No bombs, no traps, nothing. So I figured it can't be that bad so he inserts the key into the ignition.

"Tony don't do it, I have decided I want you to be the Godfather for my baby girl."

"Don't worry about it. It'll be fine. What you think it's gonna blow up or something?"

"I don't know about this Tony, there is no telling what could happen if you turn that key."

"Watch and learn, Gonzo."

Now Tony was getting kind of worried, he turned the key and gave it some gas and closed his eyes. The loudest most awful noise came from the car.

"Tony, you okay?"

He opened his eyes and his ears were ringing and he couldn't hear a thing. It was the stereo, so he turned down the volume and it just got louder. He couldn't hear a thing but noise, but the other guys heard a very loud song playing from the speakers.

"Tony get outta there."

Tony climbed out and stood back near one of the walls with the other guys. "It won't turn down. The volume it's all messed up." Guido busted out laughing.

Gonzo was irate, "Stop laughing Guido." He laughed even more. "I said stop laughing Guido." Now he was in a ball on the floor gasping for air it was so funny."

"Sorry Gonzo I can't stop laughing it's too funny."

"You wouldn't be laughing if it was your car."

Angie asked, "Is that Christina Aguilera, Beautiful?"

Gonzo shook his head, "I hate that song. Make it stop Alfie, make it stop."

Just when you thought it would go to the next song it just looped and played the same song over and over.

"Well, we better get going." Angie said as she motioned for Alfie, Christie, Guido, and Tony to go with her. "Sorry Gonzo looks like you're going to have to just drive it like that."

"Great, lets go guys."

The guys in the Christinamobile all jumped in and held their ears. They drove away and when they got to the stoplight outside Angie pulled up next to Gonzo. Gonzo looked over at Guido and the music was just blaring loud, everyone within two blocks could hear it. Guido pointed over to Gonzo and burst out laughing. Gonzo gripped the steering wheel and shook his head.

"What kind of terrorists would do something like this? This is terrible."

The music just blasted over the air waves, "You're beautiful, no matter what they say. Words can't bring me down."

One of Gonzo's guys said really loud, "Maybe they're urban terrorists."

Chapter 9

High Speed Chase

Gonzo had left when they got there and it was just Tony, Alfie, Christie, and Angie in the apartment talking. Christie and Alfie were still holding hands as they sat on the couch sipping on some hot tea.

Christie looked over at Alfie with those big brown eyes and said, "That sure was brave of you to save me like that."

"There was no way that I was just going to let you die like that, you mean to much to me. They didn't hurt you did they?"

"No, no bruises or anything. They didn't speak much English so I didn't know what all that they were saying, but I did hear them talk about Osama bin Laden a lot."

"Osama bin Laden? What I thought he was dead?"

"I heard them talking to him on their satellite phones. They were planning something and whatever it was I am sure that they wanted me dead."

"Does this have to do with Futura?"

"Yeah, they said that they bombed the Continental Flight in retaliation about some Afghan General that one of our troops assassinated."

Alfie took another sip of steaming hot tea. "When was this?"

"I'm not sure. We need to look it up on the internet."

Angie brought Christie her laptop and she went searching on the web for Afghan General assassination. "Here it is. It says that General Allabaaz of the Afghan rebels was assassinated last week in Eastern Afghanistan at Taahbag."

"So how did you decide not to get on the plane? They said that you were dead all over the news in the flight passenger list."

"When I was at the airport I was just sitting there and noticed that two Arabs were watching me. They were not wearing turbans just suits with one carry on bag. They kept on looking at me and talking on the phone. It was so loud in there I couldn't here what they were saying so I went to the bathroom came back and sat right behind them. They couldn't see me and when they found out I was gone they were talking on the phone when they called for the flight to board. That was when I heard them say my name. Then I knew that they were trying to kill me, so I just left the airport. They thought that I was on the plane and they bombed it."

"Did you know that the Senator from Texas Douglas Eisenhower was on that flight?"

"No."

"Yeah, that's why they think that the terrorists bombed it not you."

"They must have seen that I was gone and they bombed it anyway because Eisenhower was on there and you know about his anti-terrorist legislation. So they wanted to get rid of him too."

"So tell me more about this missile that you have been working on. That's why they wanted you dead isn't it?"

"Yes. The missile is known as the Afghan Cave Tactical missile or ACT missile. The chemical compound was my job and I created a chemical that spreads downward in caves and destroys oxygen molecules suffocating the people in the cave. The chemical is called..."

"Netrosia."

"Yes, netrosia, if inhaled it shuts down the lungs and can kill within minutes."

"I saw the rosebud that you left outside the room that's how we knew where you were. I did research and found several folders called the Rose and knew that you must have left it there for us to find."

"I had two cell phones and they said to throw the phone away and they saw me throwing one away in the trash but they didn't see me hide this one in my pocket. I am sure that is how you tracked me."

"That's right, Guido had a tracking app on his phone and we found you at the hotel."

"They heard you coming down the hall for me so they bailed out the window and left me there with that bomb attached to my chest. I can't thank you enough for passing their test. I don't know what I would have done without you."

"You're very welcome Christie, I would have done it for you any day."

"I am sure that they wanted all of you dead and that's why they set it up like that. So you would fail and all of you would die trying to save me."

"Their plan didn't work thank God. After this is over can I take you out? You know on a date. The date that we had planned before all of this whole mess started."

"I would like that very much, sure I would be glad to get to know you more."

Tony was watching the Fox business channel, he had several stocks that he liked to keep up with. Angie's TV was huge it was an LG 80" flatscreen OLED, posted on her living room wall. Christie was more intent on her conversation with Alfie than watching TV but she did hear something that caught her ear.

"Tony, could you turn that up a bit?"

"Sure thing what is it?"

"Just listen."

There was a man on TV talking saying, "The Sheik has agreed to allow Mustafa Hasbaland to buy the shares as a minority interest shareholder. Terraoil's stock has risen 10% since the news broke early this morning and expect's to rise even more when they launch the unveiling of their new fleet of oil tanker ships later on this week. Look for big gains in the near future for Terraoil. Moving on, Oracle's Larry Ellison has a dramatic story he is about to tell that should move up his stock as well."

"That's it. I heard them talking to a guy named Mustafa Hasbaland on the phone. He was like their boss."

"I thought Osama was their boss?"

"He is their boss too. They both tell those guys what to do. I need to get to my lab. I need to talk to my boss Susan Churchill, she needs to finish the paperwork for the missile, to get it to our defense department before it's too late."

Angie got perky and said, "I'll take you, you can come with us if you want Alfie."

"But of course, wouldn't miss it for the world."

Christie closed her laptop and put it in its bag and they all loaded themselves up in Angie's car. It was kind of breezy out and a lil' bit chilly so Angie put the top up and cranked the heater. They were off to upstate New York, but first they had to make it out of the city.

"How long of a drive is it from here?"

Christie thought for a minute, "I dunno? Put it in your GPS thingy."

Angie typed it in and there it was. "Take I-87 to Bloomington, NY approximately 2 hours and 1 minute in traffic."

"What a jewel this thing is."

"I know."

While they were crossing the Brooklyn Bridge Angie noticed that there was that same music that was from Gonzo's car, only it was coming from a van. She didn't pay much attention to it until the van pulled up next to her halfway across the bridge and they shot at her car.

Frantically Angie screamed, "Christie duck down! Alfie you okay back there?"

"Yeah."

"I know they can't catch this car."

Angie gunned it and pulled out away from them but they just sped up and tailgated her.

"Both of you stay down they could shoot again."

She sped all the way to I-87 and never saw those guys again. Alfie and Christie talked about where they wanted to go on their date for about an hour into the trip. Angie was getting anxious to get there and kept looking behind her. They were safe now, but when they shot right at Angie and she saw that bullet coming right at her car she freaked out and couldn't handle it and she kept thinking about what if they attack again.

Christie was lost in conversation with Alfie, "So you think that we would have the best dinner at Michael Jordan's Steak House?"

"Absolutely, have you ever been there?"

"No. I wonder if Angie has. Have you Angie?"

"What? Did you see that van back there. It could be following us. I think we better pull over for a bit."

"Anyway, it's right above Grand Central Station. Magnificent view, the atmosphere is eclectic I just know that you will love it. You like trains don't you?"

"My Dad used to take me on train rides during the summer all over the US. We had so much fun and we saw so many places I don't think I would have ever gotten the chance to see otherwise."

"Well, I think that you'll love it." Alfie said from the backseat sweetly dreaming of what it would be like to take her there.

The car came to a stop at a gas station about mid-way there and Angie watched as the van that she thought that was following her, harmlessly drove by. "Maybe it was just my imagination."

"You thirsty?" Alfie asked as they went into the store.

"Yeah I could use a drink."

"What do you usually drink Angie?" Christie asked as she stepped through the door that Alfie opened for them.

"Nestea."

"Ohh, that sounds good."

"I think I'll have one too."

"Why don't we just get a cold six-pack?"

"Sounds great."

They walked back outside with a bag full of groceries and a six-pack of Nestea. Angie paid for it all and she broke out a can for each of them.

"Here you go."

"Thanks Angie."

"And here's yours Christie?"

"Thank you so much. And thank you for taking us this really means a lot to me. I hope you're not too stressed out about what happened."

"No, I think it will be alright we are almost there."

They all got in the car and turned up the tunes. Christie really liked the song that was playing and she was dancing to it and singing along. "You know that they also had a TV show on Nickelodeon?"

"Didn't know that." Alfie said very interested in everything that this amazing person had to say.

"Yeah it was called the Monkees, they did skits and played their songs. Great show."

Angie was driving over the speed limit to get there faster and she had a radar detector and it wasn't going off, but there was this car up ahead going really slow that she was approaching. She looked in her rear view and there was a truck approaching fast, she would have to slow down for the car.

"Great, why do these people drive so slow?"

The truck passed her then she gunned it to get around the car only it wasn't a car it was the van. She noticed it as she passed along side it.

Christie saw it too from her side window. "Angie lookout!"

The van rammed into the side of her car, the door opened up and a taliban guy stood close to the edge. The van rammed the car again and this time the guy jumped on the back of her car and he had a knife in his hand. She swerved to try and shake him off but he had a steady grip on the roof seam.

"Press the convertible button!" Christie screamed insanely.

She pressed it and the guy went falling to the back of the car as it folded back. The terrorist guy was hanging onto the trunk seam this time and Angie swerved again but it didn't shake him away. The guy climbed up to where Alfie was sitting and hit him in the face. Alfie didn't flinch.

"Hit him back!" Christie screamed.

Alfie rared back and punched him right on the jaw. This made the guy bounce backwards and they thought he was a goner but, he managed to hang on to the trunk with one hand. Alfie scooted back and was kicking at his hand, the guy grabbed the seam with both hands and flung himself into the backseat with Alfie. They began trading punches as Angie sped away from the van. The van was about 10 yards back when Alfie hit the guy and he landed in the far corner of the seat. Alfie scooted back and when the guy stood up to grab Christie, Alfie kicked the guy right out of the car. He fell to the pavement and his van ran over him. "Bump, Bump."

All of them had lost their breath Angie noticed a road sign that said Bloomington 10 miles ahead, they were getting closer.

Alfie's face was all cut up and bleeding and Christie was hunting in the glove compartment for some napkins. She found some and climbed in the back seat as Angie closed the roof and cranked up the heat.

"My goodness, are you okay."

"I think I'll be alright. Just a flesh wound."

"Your face is battered."

"I'll be alright, but it sure is nice to have you here taking care of me."

"That guy was about to get me."

"I wasn't going to let him. Did you see me kick him out of the car?"

"Thank you, again. You are just getting in the habit of saving my life. I guess I am just going to have to save yours right back."

"You know how you could really save mine right now?"

"How?"

"With a kiss."

Christie jumped at the opportunity, hugged him and planted a big kiss right on his lips.

"Goodness you can kiss."

"Why thank you Alfie, you're not so bad yourself."

"Hey, love birds, I think we're here. Futura next exit. This it Christie?"

She stopped kissing long enough to look up and see the sign. "Yeah just turn here."

They arrived and got out of the car and noticed several armed guards at the entrances.

Chapter 10

Futura Consulting

The armed guards created a spark of emotion in Christie when she saw them as they were usually at the front gate and not at all of the entrances. As the got closer to them walking on the concrete sidewalk she asked one of them, "Everything okay?"

"Bomb threats from the Al-Qaeda terrorists, they are planning attacks. Just precautionary measures ma'am."

She had on her ID card with a Futura logo that the guards noticed and nodded to her as they passed. She swiped her card then proceeded trough the industrial green tinted front doors. There was a receptionist that was glad to see Christie, "Christie, glad to see you back, and so soon, I had heard that you were..."

"Everything's okay, I just need to speak with Susan."

"Go on through, don't forget its a casual Friday this week."

"Thanks."

The went through the security system and went on through to the main elevator. Alfie was wondering, "You don't think that the guards were there for the Continental crash do you?"

"Dunno, not sure, let's just go on up and talk to my boss, you can go with me, if you want?"

"Sure we'll go." Angie said speaking for the both of them. The elevator had FOLED walls and with the news about Terraoil on the screens. Christie had a flashback to when she was in the terrorist van and they were talking about Mustafa. With vivid imagery she recalled the looks on their faces when they found out it was Mustafa on the phone. They all went dead silent with respect and anticipation to what he was going to tell them. One of the men combed his beard as he sat straight up in his seat when he heard the faint voice on the other end of the phone.

The elevator sounded and they were at their floor and Christie awoke to her reality. "Just this way guys." They took a left down a hallway and went all the way to the end to the receptionist. There was a sharply dressed man at the desk in front of the hallway that lead back to Susan's office. "Hey Lee, Susan is expecting me."

"I'll let her know you're here."

He called her and spoke into his micro thin headset then nodded and said, "She is ready to see you. You can go on back now."

They proceeded through the hallway and saw Susan motioning for them to enter through the tinted glass. They went in and Susan jumped out of her chair and rushed over to Christie to give her a hug. "I am so glad you're okay, Christie sit down."

Before they sat Chrisite introduced them to her boss. "Alfie, Angie, this is Susan Churchill Vice President of Futura Biotech division. They all shook hands and sat as Christie said, "Alfie is a programmer for TechOne, and Angie owns Traccia's in Manhattan. They are both good friends of mine and we had to see you as soon as possible."

"Christie, I am just so glad that you're alive. Goodness, how did you not get on that plane?"

"Long story short, I noticed the terrorists and left the boarding area as everyone was getting on the plane before they noticed that I was gone."

"Oh Christie, thank God you are okay."

Christie handed Susan a thumb drive with a serious expression and she immediately plugged it into her laptop. Christie then brushed her hair back and said, "Everything is on it, we need to get this authorized for production."

"Oh, I guess you don't know then do you. We have already began production on the Netrosia and sent the Air Force the first shipment. They already had over 100 blank missiles ready for the containers. MicroTech had everything installed and everything was going according to plan until they hit a wall with the software. There was some sort of glitch and they have got MicroTech working on it as we speak. They had scheduled the first strike for tomorrow, but now it looks like it could be another few weeks before they get everything worked out."

"What?...I mean that's great that we already got the Netrosia approved. I had no idea. There is something else we need to talk about."

"Sure, anything Christie."

"Okay, the people that took me captive are working for Osama bin Laden and this other guy Mustafa Hasbaland. I just saw on the news today that this Mustafa has just bought shares of the stock Terraoil and he must be planning something. What, I don't know, that is why I was wondering if you could do some CIA research for me. I know you know people at Langley so could you just check this out for me and get back with me."

"Sure Christie, I'll get whatever intel they have on him and this new acquistion. I should have it by the end of the day."

"That would be great." Christie reaches out and takes a card from Susan's desk and writes something on the back and hands it to Susan and says, "This is where you can reach me. Send whatever you get to this address."

"Is there anything else Christie?"

"No..."

Alfie took Christie by the arm as they were walking out and said, "Actually, if I could talk to Christie for a minute."

"What is it?" Christie sweetly asked as if he was interrupting the meeting.

"Listen, about a month ago I worked on a project at TechOne for MicroTech called the ACT GS and I think that I can help with the glitch. I was responsible for programming the Satellite relay, I know everything there is to know about that project and if there was anybody that could help the Air Force right now it would be me."

"Wait up. Are you saying that we were working on the same project here?"

"Yes I think so."

"And you can fix the problem with the software?"

"Yes, that is precisely what I am saying."

"Out of all of the hundreds of guys that emailed me on Matchmate, I pick you. God must have really been at work getting us together like He did."

"Yeah, I guess so. Listen tell Susan that she can send me over there."

They step back inside her office and Alfie asks her, "Do you know what their problem was with the software?"

Susan responded, "They didn't say, we're just BioTech over here."

Christie interjected, "Alfie programmed the software, well at least some of the software for the ACT missile."

Susan responded, "Would you be willing to go over there and work on it with the Air Force?"

"Sure, I was going to ask you the same thing."

"Let me make a call." Susan got patched over to the Air Force weapons development lab and got all of the information for Alfie. They asked to speak with him and Susan handed over the phone.

"Yes, this is Alfred, Alfred von Monk."

"And you're the programmer of some of the components of the software for the ACT GS?"

"Yeah I did all of the Satellite relay."

"Its not the Satellite relay that we are having trouble with it's the propulsion system, its not in sync with the guidance system."

"Yeah, that was Eric that programmed that part he works under me and I instructed him on how to get it to work right. I guess he didn't get everything straight."

"Well I think you could help us. Could you be here tomorrow by 8:00am?"

"Where are you located?"

"Rome, New York. Its the Air Force Research lab Griffiss Air Force Base."

"I'll be there with some help from my friends." The call ended and he was all smiles and showed his gratitude to Susan, "I can't thank you enough Mrs. Churchill you have been wonderful and I hope we can get these missiles launched before anything happens."

"My thoughts exactly. Well I hope you can get some things fixed over there tomorrow, it's a great facility. I'll have Lee walk you to the front."

Chapter 11

Griffiss

It was a beautiful day there in Rome, New York Angie was kinda wishing that Tony had made the trip with them but she was sure that he was giving the waitresses all they could handle back at Traccia's. Griffiss Air Force Base was a very large facility with hangars all over the place. At 8:00 in the morning it was clear skies and it looked like a great day for some programming and maybe a trip in the sky.

There was a A-10 Thunderbolt being armed with all kinds of missiles that was on the ground next to the research hangar when they got there. Their guide was a fighter pilot that was shot down in the gulf war and barely made it out of there alive. Alfie wanted to know more about the missile so he asked the guide, "Doyle, which one of these warbirds will the missile be launched from?"

Doyle, "Aggie" Conan dusted off the shoulder of his fighter suit and said, "You can call me Aggie, everyone else around here does. Well, that's a very good question there sport. There are only a few attack planes that actually launch missiles like the ACT and the one we will be using is the Thunderbolt. We can strap on about 10 on each bird. I'm thinking 10 is all that we'll need to get those bastards outta there. Who knows we might even get Osama Bin Laden."

Angie typing a tweet on her phone, was curious about some things and asked, "Hey Aggie, what are the chances of us getting Osama?"

"Well there, sweet thang, the last video of Osama that towel head coward bastard, was filmed back in 2006 and we haven't heard anything, not a pip or a squeak, since then. He could be anywhere out there. Hell, he could even be dead already for all that we know. We've got the best intelligence in all of the world with the CIA and you'd think that by now we'd have already got the coward, but nope, he's still out there and I think, to answer your question there sweety, that we got a pretty good chance of getting him with this missile. He's gotta be hiding out in one of those caves in the Afghanistan mountains and if he is in there we'll get him."

Christie was texting Susan about the facilities and overheard the conversation as they were all walking to the research lab. "What is the chances of this missile ending the war on terror?"

"Sugar, I don't know if we'll ever really end the war on terror. We might get Osama, but he has already trained all those Al-Qaeda coward towel heads and those guys are everywhere, all over the world not just Afghanistan. We might make a pretty big dent in their operations if we kill Osama, but there will always be those who defy authority and rebel against those in power. If they find out that their leader is dead it could cripple their morale and they could retreat, but you never know they could just retaliate with more attacks on the US. You never know."

Alfie just text over to Christie, "I sure do hope that I can fix this missile.(Rose)" He ended it with a rose emoticon.

She sent a text back saying, "I know you can Alfie, I know you can. ;)"

Aggie and the crew were already to the lab and he said, "Well, looks like you guys have some work to do. I was going to tell you earlier Alfred, there is someone here to meet you that will help with your project."

Aggie motioned towards the man with his back facing them at a desk in the office area. Angie texted Christie, "I wonder who this is?" The man in the blue jumpsuit at a type writer handed a piece of typed paper to a Fed Ex man and said get this out to everyone.

When he did he saw the group out of the corner of his eye and said, "Alfred? Is that you?"

"Dad? What the? Goodness its been a while. So they sent you over here today did they?"

"Alfred, you seem to be doing pretty well for yourself, you have these stunningly beautiful ladies with you. What did you do win the lottery?"

Christie said, "Thank you."

"The pleasure is all mine my sweet dear." Chandler said kissing her hand.

"No Dad I am here to help with the programming."

"They said you'd be here so I decided to come over and see if I could help you out in any way. I'm doing it for you and for this country."

"Thanks Dad."

Chandler Monk finished typing another paper and said, "Send this out to everyone."

Alfred responded, "You're still sending messages on typed paper that typewriter looks like its from the 1940's. Have you ever heard of texting and email, maybe twitter or facebook?"

"Dad, have you never heard of email?"

"I'm just messing with you." Chandler pulls out his Sprint Samsung Epic. "This thing is 4G you know what that means?"

"Yeah its the speed of the net..."

"It means it's 4 Grown ups only. You couldn't handle a phone like this Callahan."

"Maybe that's why then sent you to desk duty."

"What? I turned in my weapons but, I'll never turn in this bad bagel."

"There are all kind of perks working for the Air Force son. Like this Scroll Laptop. It's the size of a small cylinder that fits in your hand or in your case your purse. And... it's got a flexible screen and keyboard that scroll out and flip up. It's the latest technology."

"Okay, now I want one of those."

"Not gonna do it. Wouldn't be prudent." He said in his best George Bush accent. "Why haven't you introduced me to these incredible ladies?"

"Dad, this is Christie and Angelica, this is my Dad, Chandler."

"Ladies, it is my pleasure. You must tell me all about yourselves. So how do you know Alfred?"

Christie started out, "I'll take this one. Mr. Chandler..."

"Call me Chan. And are you single?"

"Well, Chan, yes I am kind of."

"I am sure that Alfred is single ya'll ought to get together."

"Actually we've been dating. Alfred and I met on Matchmate.com and I fell for him the moment that we met. He has already saved my life I don't know how many times and every chance I get I save his right back with a kiss. Your son is quite the romantic."

"See Dad, I'm not all ones and zeroes."

"You know he takes after me, I was a regular Don Juan back in the day."

"He most certainly has, and now he is about to save us all again with this program that he is going to fix."

"Yeah, so we better be going thanks for all the romance stories Dad."

"I want to hear more of his stories."

"Let me tell you the story of how I met his mother, its so romantic. I got some family photos together and some flowers and took them to the amnesia ward at the hospital and found the most beautiful woman that couldn't remember anything. We got married a few weeks later and we had Alfred 9 months after that. Of course I had to remind her of anniversaries and holidays."

Angie didn't know what to think. "That's...great Chan."

Alfie doesn't like for him to tell that story so he said, "I know it sounds horrible, it's the only way anyone would marry the guy. I love my mom and thank God the amnesia was temporary. Not really, they met in the Amazon."

"She was the most beautiful amazon woman, she had a bone in her hair and a bone in her nose, quite stunning. I wanted her and she wanted me, but the chief wanted something in return. We all had a big party and I was taking pictures of them with my Polaroid camera, B-L-E-W their mind. They had never even seen themselves in a mirror much less a picture. Needless to say his mom and I flew out of there back to the states and the Chief had setup shop as a photographer making family portraits of the tribesmen. Bones and all, I still keep this picture of his mom when she had a bone in her nose. So romantic."

Christie thought it was hilarious and did her best not to laugh, "Romantic indeed."

Chandler looked at the women with a real serious look and they burst out laughing. Angie asked, "How did y'all really meet Chan?"

"Playing basketball."

"Here he goes again, and let me guess she could dunk?"

"No really, she had her mind made up that she told God that she would marry the first man that could beat her playing basketball and I did. Six months later Alfred was born."

"Six months, sorry Chan but I think that one of those players beat you to her."

"I didn't tell you, Alfred is half black last name is Abdual Jabar, aww I love him anyway. At first his mom and I thought about renigging, we kept him anyway, cutest black baby you ever saw. Then as he grew up we gave him white man's pills and now he looks completely normal. You could never tell that once he was as black as President Obama."

"Alfred." Christie said. It was all that she could say.

"No really, it was nine months."

The women just laughed and laughed.

Aggie was still standing around listening to everyone and finally said, "Well, I think that we better get this show on the road. Ya'll ready to fix this program?"

Alfie still distraught by his dad telling the story said, "Ready as I'll ever be."

"Get your laptop there Chan. Alfie, ladies this way." Aggie showed them the way around to the offices to where the software lab was. In the programers room there were about ten laptop stations and Aggie sat Alfie and Chandler down right next to each other, while Aggie took the seat next to them.

Aggie instructed them in how they should go about correcting the problem. "Okay guys, I am no expert and that is why we have gathered you here today. I want for Alfie to work on the receiver and Chandler can work on the transmitter. Here is the problem area, any questions let me know."

He pointed out the areas on the screen of the code that needed to be fixed. After about an hour they both had the problem fixed and it was ready for testing. Alfie spoke up when he was done, "Okeedokee, got mine what about you there pops?"

"Mine has finished the simulations, I think its ready to go as well."

Aggie was pleased and said, "I guess we can go test out this new addition on one of the Thunderbolts. First to the missiles, this way guys."

Aggie took the SD cards out of their laptops and lead them down the hall to where the missiles were stored. He walked up to the target missile and inserted both SD cards and uploaded the new fixed programs and then he called out to one of the technicians, "Hey there Poe! We need this poquito vato on the Thunderbolt. Comprende?"

"I don't know who you talkin to I aint Poe, I'm B. Roaker, Al Roaker's son."

"Well then, where did Poe go?"

"He's been in the bathroom for the last hour. Sounds like he might be passin a stone or something."

"Can you do this? We need this installed."

"Aww man, I don't know, you know that's Poe's job. I'm just a broke mechanic."

"Can you go get Poe?"

"I'm busy gotta get this done today."

"Alright I'll go in and get him."

Aggie went over to the bathrooms and looked under the stall and saw Poe's pants around his boots then he heard these screams, "Yessss! Way to go! That's it! Who's tha man!"

"Poe, you okay?"

"Oh, I'm great."

"What are you screaming about?"

"Can't say."

"Come one you can tell me."

"I can't talk about it."

"Charles said that you were passing a stone. Is that right?"

"He sure can pass the rock."

"So you passed a stone?"

"No. Is he crazy or what?"

"Can you come out of there?"

"Yeah."

Poe pulled his pants up and opened the stall and walked out then he pocketed his phone.

"I just made $10,000."

"You're going to sell the stone?"

"Stone? What are you talking about, my basketball team just won. I was watching it on my cell phone, don't tell the boss though."

"I won't. Listen we need you to install the new ACT missile."

"Yeah sure thing."

He had this special lift that would bring the missile up to the attachment point on the jet. He loaded it up then drove it over to the Jet and attached it to the section underneath the wings. "It's attached. Are you guys going to go and bomb some Afghan's today?"

Aggie responded, "Well, we have to test it first."

"When you do bomb the hell outta those Al-Qaeda bastards."

"We will do our best." One of the pilots said as he jumped up into the cockpit of the A-10 Thunderbolt.

Aggie said to the pilot, "We just need a test launch for the ACT GS."

"Got it."

"We all need to go back to the hangar so he can take off."

Alfie said, "Sure thing there Aggie, I think that his one is going to work."

They backed up to the viewing area and heard the jet engines start up with a loud thunder. The jet took off the runway and then circled back and fired the missile. The missile didn't have the Netrosia installed yet or they all could be toast so he fired a blank missile to test the adjustments done to the software.

The ACT missile sailed through the air and Alfie and Christie took a deep breath as it hit the target. Alfie let out a glaring, "Yes, we did it."

Christie looked up to Alfie with those gorgeous brown eyes and took his hand and said, "Goodness Alfie, I had no idea you were so versatile."

"Comes with the territory ma'am." Said Alfie in his best John Wayne accent.

Chandler looked over to Alfie and said, "In all seriousness I am proud of you son. You did a great job with that program."

"Hey, so did you Dad. Proud of you too."

Aggie was ecstatic that it worked and said, "I want to thank all of you, excellent job there guys. Alfie and Chandler on the software and Christie on the Netrosia great job I can't tell you how pleased I am and the President will be as well when he hears that we got the missile working. I have some phone calls to make so ya'll just hang around."

Aggie made calls to his superiors and Angie called Tony to let him know that they would be on their way pretty soon.

Aggie was done and they all were waiting to hear what would happen next. "I talked to my superiors and they said that we will be arming the missiles with the Netrosia and the new software and a squadron of Thunderbolts will be going to Afghanistan today."

Christie was so excited, "That's great."

Aggie paced around for a bit kind of reluctant to say something like he was searching for the right words or something and then he said, "They want to know if you want to go to Afghanistan with us to watch the missiles be launched? We have a Globemaster jet that is taking several of us over there and ya'll can come if you want."

Christie asked Angie, "Can you be gone from Traccia's this long?"

"Yeah, I think it will be okay. I better tell Tony."

Alfie was all about it, "Sure I'll go, what about you Dad?"

"I don't know."

Christie encouraged him, "It will be great to see our missile at work."

"Yeah, I guess so."

Aggie summed up the mission. "We will leave here in an hour after all of the jets are armed and ready. The Globemaster will be here to pick us up pretty soon, you can eat on board if you're hungry."

Chapter 12

Rhiyad Saudi Arabia

They were in the meeting room of the Sheik at his palace and Mustafa was watching the screen of all of the ships that the Sheik had. "Is there a tanker for every port city in the United States?"

The Sheik was sipping his drink and responded, "Naw."

There was a video of a tanker on the screen that showed its interior and exterior design. First was the schematics then it went to a full scale model, next it was an actual ship. Mustafa got a good idea of where all of the ships were capable of going and also of what they looked like. "Is oil and gas the only thing that it can transport?"

"Not at all there are sections of the ship, as you see here, that also ship many other items."

"Excellent."

Mustafa was very pleased to see such a a versatile ship and it was obvious to him that he made the right decision in choosing to side with the Sheik.

Chapter 13

HINDUKUSH MOUNTAINS, AFGHANISTAN

Deep underground underneath the Hindukush mountains of Afghanistan was one of the Al-Qaeda bases that was still in operation. Some call them caves but the Al-Qaeda Jihad rebels called it Kudesh which was their code word for refuge base. These scoundrels consisted of about 40 men who were very loyal to their leaders Osama bin Laden and Mustafa Hasbaland. They worked tirelessly under their rule and would stop at nothing to see that their orders were carried out.

Yesterday a group of American soldiers had raided their village near their base of Kudesh where their families lived. Some of their wives were brought into American arms and taken for interrogations. The Jihad rebels were extremely angry at this and were planning a mission to capture their wives back from the Americans. This was just what the Americans wanted and as they planned the rebels found ways to subterfuge their attack by using American Army uniforms.

While putting on these uniforms deep underground the rebels found some American magazines to know what they should look like. Their leader Tapesh called out to TiHusha, "Ti, did you know that Brittney Spears boobs are silicone?" He said this in the funniest Indian Afghan accent, that is how they both talked.

"That is incredible they look so real in all of her concerts, they bounce when she jumps and they jiggle when she moves, I would have never known."

"I am very wise I know these things." Tapesh combed his beard and acted as if he exuded intelligence.

"And how do you know these things?" TiHusha held out his arms in questioning.

"Star magazine had a whole article about her implants." Tapesh's index finger shot into the air.

"So you steal you're wife's magazines and know these things. Is there anything that you don't steal?" Tihusha shrugged and reached for a magazine.

"Yes there is." Tapesh's eyebrow raised and looked like a loading ramp that they got nuclear weapons from being a unibrow and all.

"And what might that be?" Tihusha now had a Star magazing in his hands and shot his eyes toward Tapesha just above the top of the magazine.

"Kisses." Tpaesh delicately said as his eyelashes fluttered.

"Really?" Rolling his eyes Tihusha's lips went back and his nostrils flared.

"Don't go Saturday Night Live on me now." Tapesh threw down a magazine and acted disgusted.

"Really?" There, he did it again.

"You're doing it, keep it up and I have a toilet ring with your name on it. You know that show is not nearly as funny as Mad TV." Tapesh points directly at the Tihusha, who is sitting in a cheap chair under a light bulb, then points away.

"You know that guy in *%$# My Dad Says is on Mad TV?" Tihusha sits up in the wooden chair then places the magazine on the rickety table next to him.

"Yes he is very humorous. You know you would be great on TV or on stage." Tapesh's eyes were searching for the word.

"The last time that I was on stage it changed my life forever."

"What happened?"

"I was in Coonya Mexico on a vacation and I got asked to hold a plastic bag for a horse on stage. It changed my life forever."

"Now that is humorous."

"The word is funny knucklehead." Tihusha leans over to tie his boots.

"Don't go PTI on me here Mike Wilbon." Tapesh stands with a fist and some spit shot out of his mouth as he was saying PTI and it landed in Tihusha's eye.

Wiping the launched saliva out of his eye Tihusha says, "What? It is a very funny term, the knucklehead that you are."

"You want some T & A?"

"From you? I think I'll pass."

"On a turkey and alvacado sandwich?"

"Oh for a minute there I thought you'd be asking me for some bologna and jam."

Tapesh squinted his eyes and began to walk in a circle in his new American uniform, "You know how I get kisses without stealing them?"

"Let me guess...It involves guns. Am I right?"

"What? Now you are the knucklehead Tony Kornheiser. No, actually I said to her the other day, 'Honey you put the rump in scrumptious.' And boom she was kissing all over me."

"Oh yeah, well I got one for you, you are such a great military leader and all. You put the sass in assassin."

"What? There is no sass in my assassinating I am all man." Tapesh stomps his boots in the dirt.

"Well then tell me this Mr. all man. Who tucks in their shirt under their panties. Your granny panties are showing evil dictator."

Tapesh pulls his underwear up with the label out, "These are Hanes for men not Hanes her way. That is what my wife wears."

With a stern lip TiHusha said, "Whatever, you still put the sass in assassin."

Tapesh snaps his fingers like an African American sista and moves his arms all about. "Enough! There is no sass in anything I do."

"Sure, Whoopie."

"I do not look like Whoopie Goldberg, Tihush."

"You sure do have her sass though."

Another rebel soldier walks in the room and says, "More like ShaNanae."

"If anything I am like Martin Lawrence."

"Martin Lawrence by day and ShaNanae by night."

"I am leaving, I will get you guys back, and I will have my way."

TiHusha snaps his fingers like Tapesh moving his arms all about and said, "ShaNanae says its Hanes her way or the highway."

Karush the other rebel soldier stomped his boots in the dirt and started walking the other direction mocking Tapesh. "Shananae don't play that. I'll get you guys back."

TiHusha burst out laughing at Karush slapping his knee as dust flew from his used American uniform. Karush did an about face before he got to the door then Tapesh slammed the door behind himself on the other side of the room. Karush then said to TiHusha, "ShaNanae is in a hissy fit."

TiHusha shook his head and said, "Must have got his Hanes her way in the wrong way."

"Doesn't he know by now the skinny side goes in the front?"

Very frankly TiHusha ducked his head and looked up at Karush and said, "You would think so my friend, you would think so."

They both then kicked back and sat around the table and popped open an Afghan soda. Karush sparked with an idea, "You know that Christmas is just around the corner?"

TiHusha took out his phone and said, "Yes, I have a calendar. The best time of the year."

"I was thinking, you know how Dan Quail misspelled potato and he was their vice president, well how is it that those crazy American don't misspell things on their Christmas lights like Ho Ho Ho and not Hoe Hoe Hoe."

Tihusha sipped and wiped his mouth and said, "Do you know why Santa is so jolly? It's because he knows where all the bad girls live."

Karush was laughing so hard his side started hurting. "Good one my friend. What do you think Santa does the rest of the year in his sleigh, you know that it says 'Love Machine' on the side in the off season."

"And what toys does Santa make in the offseason? He's got this whole factory of elves that make stuff do they just sit around and drink eskimo beer? So what kind of toys do they make?"

With a smile Karush combed his beard, "The good kind my friend, the good kind."

TiHusha had another good one, "And the North pole? Have you ever been to Santa's north pole? How do you know that it isn't some kind of big stripper's pole for all of the naughty bad girls that he picks up in his sleigh?"

Karush gulped down the rest of his soda and responded, "Santa has his own strip club up there called, 'Santa's Naughty and Oh That's Nice Gentleskimo's club."

TiHusha had to know, "So what are you getting for Christmas?"

"Underwear." Karush reclutantly said in a deep tone.

Tihusha had a vision, "Don't be like Tapesh and wear Hanes her way with the skinny side in back."

To make sure that he knew what kind Karush said, "Oh no, my friend, my wife always gets me briefs."

Tihusha remebered what a friend of his had once told him, "You know why they call them briefs right?"

"Tell me oh great one."

"Because when you're with your wife they are only on very briefly. Or if its your situation and you've been married forever then they're briefly off."

With satisfaction Karush said, "Mark Buerhle."

"What? Is that who she has been seeing when I am away?"

"Perfect my friend. He had a perfect game. Now that I think about it, I thought it was because they knew that sex is always so brief with my wife."

Taking him very seriously, "That might be the reason, they probably knew hundreds of years ago when the inventor Michael Jordan would invent the Hanes briefs that you, my friend, would have brief sex. Sounds logical."

"You know why they call them boxers?"

"Why?"

"Because when your wife is with you, you will never put up a fight if she wants them off."

"72 Dolphins."

"What?"

"Perfect again my friend."

"I want a new phone for Christmas one like Mustafa or Osama has... the Samsung Epic."

"Oh goodness so do I, I could text to my thumbs delight."

TiHusha had his new windows phone out and sent a text to Karush. "You are such a good friend...TGFU."

Karush typed back, "TGFU too."

"What does that stand for?"

"It stands for pride and the American way...what do you think it stands for? Thank God For You."

"Shouldn't you say TGFY?"

"Right."

"It just sounded like you were saying Thank God FU."

"Well we are about ready for this mission and hopefully we will see our wives soon so TGIF and TGFU."

It was about 1:00 in the morning and they were all getting ready for the siege to take back their wives. Tapesh had all of the men gathered around in the main dining room with tons of tables and chairs, there had to be at least 40 of the rebel soldiers in attendance. There was one table at the front of the room where Tapesh was sitting with TiHusha next to his side and they were talking about something, some kind of strategy I suppose. Then Tapesh stood up on top of the table and began to give a speech.

He screamed at first, "Men! Silence!" They all just kept on talking to a medium roar. Fury raged within Tapesh and he grabbed an AK 47 from the table and fired off a few rounds into the dirt ceiling. Dust sparkled falling into the shafts of the ceiling lights. Instantly they all quieted down and he got their attention.

"Now that I have your attention we need to make some things clear about our mission tonight. Here is what we are going to do..."

Tapesh and about 10 of the others including Tihusha and Karush were jogging to their position in the pitch black night. The air was brisk and stung against the cooled sweat on their foreheads. They had been running for at least 10 minutes by now and they were all sweating like Roseanne Barr on a treadmill, only they weren't eating any twinkies, just carrying their guns and about 80 pounds of ammo and other stuff on their backs.

They were a good 13 miles south of the US Army base and they stopped to check their coordinates, and for a breather too. Tapesh had his pocket GPS Magellen and he was scanning the beautiful surroundings in the valley as the moon appeared out from the constant cloud cover. They were in a valley in between two steep mountains on each side. Tapesh had a ureka moment, "I've got it."

The wise guy Karush said, "Good, now can we go I am freezing out here its about to snow any minute."

"We will welcome the snow like a kiss from the gods. The road is very close and we must find it quick. The snow will cover our tracks. This way men. They all took off running in a Northwest direction when a moon lit glittering snowflake caught his eye and flittered and fluttered to land on Tapesh's shoulder. Immediately after the snow started coming down hard and they were all pleased to see that their tracks were being covered. With Tapesh's next stride he kicked up some dirt mixed in with the snow.

"This is it guys, the road, alright, we must hide just over there in the bushes, but first we prepare the bait. TiHusha you ready?"

Reluctantly he said, "Yes, can we get on with it."

"Alright Karush go position yourself on that ridge and tell us when you see them. If they are on schedule they should be in our sights in a four minutes."

By now they were all covered in snow and TiHusha was ready as were all of the men standing by waiting on the order. Karush got bored so he started catching snowflakes with his tongue and after a few landed he heard a noise far off in the distance. He scrambled for his binoculars, adjusted them and got a confirming view of lights about a mile away. Again he bumbled around for his two way and pressed in and heard the click, "I just spotted them, they are about a mile away."

"Good work Karush, stay there and we'll pick you up in a minute."

Tapesh motioned to TiHusha and he took off the arm of his jacket and underneath there was much blood and gauze wrapped around his bicep. He began limping trodding through the snow. When the transport truck got there they pulled up beside him to make sure that he was one of theirs, that's when TiHusha hit the ground. About four guys in the front of the truck jumped out rubber to snow and went to see if their soldier was alright.

All of them were wearing US Army digi's and TiHusha had blood all over the soft white snow. It was dark red around the impact point where his arm landed and then the snow soaked in the rest leaving a pink ring outline. It looked kind of like a fresh made Tiger's Blood Hawaiian shaved ice. The C.O. Spoke up first, "You alright there soldier?"

TiHusha just groaned, "UGGGHHH!"

Immediately the CO called out to the truck, "Everyone out, and bring a stretcher! Stat! Kerry bring your stuff this guy is hurt pretty bad."

They all crawled out of there like a Chinese fire drill, there were 6 in all and just when they were all on the snow Tapesh and the rest of them plowed out from behind the bushes. Tapesh got in the driver's seat as TiHusha swiftly pulled out his gun and pointed at the CO. The other guys each had green dots on the rest of the truck transport crew. The US soldiers were surrounded, they put down their weapons and the rebel soldiers kept a steady aim of green dots on each of the US soldiers foreheads.

Slowly they backed away into the vehicle, Tapesh knew that they were a good 13 miles south of the Army base and it would take them a gallywander to get back there in the cold snow. What he wasn't sure of was their communications equipment. He got out of the truck and pointed his AK 47 at the CO and said, "Your equipment, take it all off and place it in the back of the truck."

The CO didn't want to do that because he knew that it was his only way of getting the word out to their base to call for help. Reluctantly he relinquished his communication equipment and placed it next to their weapons in the back of the truck.

Now Tapesh's worries were gone he knew that the objective was complete and they had many more on the way if they were going to see their wives ever again. Tapesh turned the truck around and about a mile up the road was Karush sitting on the side of the road with his head in the air and his tongue hanging out. Just as he caught the biggest sparkling snowflake on his tongue he saw their lights and closed his mouth. He stood up and got out in the center of where he thought that the road was, the snow had already covered the trucks tracks, and waved his arms.

Tapesh saw him and slowed when he arrived. "Get in the back Karush, there is a heater back there."

Tapesh could see Karush start to climb in so he gunned it and Karush fell getting a mouthful of snow in his mouth. Tapesh stopped allowing him to get close enough to the back of the truck then he gunned it again. The guys in the back were laughing so hard that their sides hurt.

Tihusha yelled out, "Just get in Karush, quit playing around."

"Quit speeding off."

"No really you can get in this time." So Karush walked up to the truck and grabbed onto the edge of the gate. It was a large transport truck that had a tin cover open in the back with a small gate that unlatched to let the soldiers up the tire and on the steps to the back seats. Just as Karush was about to jump up Tapesh sped off. This left Karush facedown in the snow again.

TiHusha asked, "What is your problem? Just get in my friend."

In the rear view mirror Tapesh saw not only Karush but the US Soldiers running to catch up with them, he had to do something fast. Karush jumped in and cuddled up to the heater. The fastest one of the bunch was Kerry the EMT running in a dead heat and before Tapesh could slam on the gas Kerry latched onto the back gate. Tapesh punched it and they sped off with Kerry's boots dragging the ground.

He attempted to pull himself up on the gate, but TiHusha, shaking in the cold, kicked at his hands. Kerry repositioned himself and grabbed onto the tire beneath the gate and now his knees were hitting every bump of caleche rock underneath the snow. Kerry the resilient one hiked up his boots to grasp on the huge truck tire and now his jacket was picking up snow as it grazed the top of the road.

TiHusha yelled out, "Karush get over here." Karush gave up his seat at the furnace and went to the back of the truck and looked out over the gate. All they saw was a tire. TiHusha radioed to Tapesh, "He's gone."

They were now going about 60 miles an hour, Tapesh wished he could go faster but the snow was too thick and they could hit an ice patch and go skidding off the road. He kept it at 60 and they trucked onward to the base. Kerry had no idea what he was going to do next but he knew he couldn't hold on for much longer so he climbed his way back up top the gate without them seeing him and climbed in and grabbed for TiHusha's gun. Everyone in the back started screaming, so Karush walked back to where the action was and Kerry had a gun pointed right at TiHusha. Karush hiked up his leg and kicked Kerry right in the chest and Kerry went sailing back out of the truck and he got off a shot at TiHusha right before he hit the snow.

"Are you alright?" Karush was searching for where the bullet hit him.

TiHusha let out a groan and said, "I got hit." TiHusha doubled over in pain grabbing his bicep. He was bleeding but you couldn't tell how bad because it was on the same arm with all of the goats blood with the gauze.

Karush yelled around to anyone, "We need some water back here quick. He's been shot."

One of the guys brought some bottled water to him and Karush poured it over his arm. Pretty soon you could see where the bullet hit him. It barely grazed his shoulder and there was a small amount of blood seeping out.

TiHusha was in pain and wondered, "Am I going to make it? OHHH the pain!"

Karush decided to play along, "I think you might have a few more minutes, you're bleeding pretty bad it must have hit an artery. Is there something you want for us to tell your wife?"

With his good arm TiHusha pulled an envelope out of his front jacket pocket. "Give her this, it's a letter. ARGGGH! The pain!"

"Keep pressure on the wound he is bleeding bad." Karush pressed in on the spot where the bullet nicked him.

"Well it was nice knowing you TiHusha, sorry you couldn't be there to give her this letter yourself. You were tough..."

Samoosh was sitting across and noticed what was going on here and he said, "And brave, you were a great soldier."

"ARGGGHHH! I cant take it. The pain."

"Don't fade on us we might can get there in time for a paramedic."

Samoosh said, "Wasn't that guy that shot him a paramedic?"

Karush said to TiHusha, "Just stay with us. If you see the light go towards it."

"UGGGHH!"

Now Karush wanted to pull a fast one on him, "TiHusha did you love your wife?"

"UGGG! Yes, she is very beautiful."

"Would you mind if I dated her after you're dead?"

This really shook him up, "What? No, you bastard!"

"Well she is a very good looking woman and I was just thinking that after you're dead and all that we might could hook up. That's all."

"No, you evil bastard how could you do that to me?"

Now Karush was really laying it on thick. "She does have a nice rack."

Samoosh got in on it too, "Yeah she does. Some tata's for the Samoosh."

Tapesh yelled to the guys in the back, "Alright we are one mile away, bring me the radio equipment."

Kartoof saw what was going on and was sitting next to Karush. "Listen TIHusha they are just yanking your chain man. You're not going to die. The bullet barely hit you. Look for yourself."

"What? I am not going to die?" TiHusha moved the gauze away and saw a small nick with no blood. "You bastards, I am gonna get you guys for this. You're dead."

With Tapesh in the drivers seat they approached the gate and he radioed in for them to open the gates. Once the gates were open they drove in past a few coyote brown buildings and tents and pulled to the right and parked the truck. The truck was behind one of the brown buildings and in a dimly lit area where they all got out and found the entrance to where their wives were being held.

They opened the door to a very large room that served as barracks for the women and they were all asleep. There was one soldier that was asleep in the beds next to them and Tapesh whispered as fog emitted from his mouth, "Be quiet don't wake this one. Find your wife and wake her and lets get the heck outta here."

Slowly and methodically they made their way through the room waking up all the women minute they were all back in the back of the truck huddled around the heater pulling out of there. No lights, as Tapesh started the engine. They drove off and through the front gates without waking any of the Army soldiers that were in the base. There was much jubilation in the back as there were hugs for everyone. In an hour they were back to their small town and in their houses cheering for their escape to freedom.

All of them men stayed the rest of the night and the next day with their wives in their town and headed out later on that afternoon just before it was getting dark.

Chapter 13

THE GLOBEMASTER

Flight to Sabzwar Afghanistan

The skies were clear in a brisk air that was tailor made for trekking across the globe. The crew was inside playing cards when Aggie, outside and talking to the pilots, first saw the Globemaster come into sight just south of the base. Like a groundhog Aggie popped his head inside the hangar and yelled out to the crew, "It's here, get your stuff! We're going to Afghanistan."

Aggie described the jet to the crew as they were walking out to load up, "The C-17 Globemaster III can transport 134 passengers or troops or about 100 airline passenger seats capacity. In war it could carry 54 ambulatory patients with a team of doctors and nurses. It is the largest transport jet of the US Air Force." It was quite a sight to see as the crew came billowing out of the hangar to find it had landed and was ready to pick them up.

As soon as the giant jet taxied up on the strip its large back ramp was deployed and a team of soldiers sprinted out to man their stations. One of the soldiers walked up to Aggie and the crew and said, "I hear y'all are in need of a lift."

Aggie was glad to see the man that had just emerged from the ramp, "General, its been years. You heading this flight?"

"Yes sir, y'all get loaded up and we'll catch up on everything."

Last night at the hotel Angie had taken the opportunity to go to the local mall and get some new clothes, one getup, of which she was wearing which included a short plaid skirt, green long sleeve silk blouse and a short sweater. She was looking quite hot but not to be outmatched by the gorgeous Christie who was wearing some skin tight jeans that really complimented her figure when Alfie wasn't, and Aggie had given her an Air Force t-shirt that fit her brilliant breasts perfectly.

With their bags and purses in their hands they made the ascent up the ramp to their seats like only a beautiful woman can. Christie sat next to Alfie and across the aisle Chandler next to Angie. Aggie and General Watson followed up and proceeded to the front row of seats. Alfie was sitting there strapped in wondering if his compliments to Christie had made any impression on her and her lips were about the only other thing on his mind.

With the back ramp up and all fastened in the powerful thrusts of the jet kicked in and Alfie and Christie felt the G's of takeoff. There had to be someway that Alfie could get a kiss on this flight, goodness everyone saw her eyes towards him while they were playing cards. What did it take to get a kiss? Saving her life? The best part was when she saved him right back with a glorious kiss and that sort of thing was what Alfie was looking forward to. This situation wasn't the norm in dating relationships, he thought, or was it something better? Saving her from terrorists isn't the usual, "And that's how I met your mother," speech.

He wanted to thank her for the kiss goodnight at the hotel. Well, it was more than just a kiss, there was passion in that one, and this only heightened his passion that he had in his heart for her. The real question now, on his mind was what were her feelings for him.

The Globemaster jet was now at cruising altitude and Aflie wanted to somehow share what he felt for her, "Where did you learn to play cards like that? You should be on TV for hearts. If there were a hearts tournament."

He couldn't. He just didn't know where to start, but he knew that compliments could be a starting point. Christie as graceful as she was said, "You know you're not so bad yourself. I couldn't have won that game without those cards that you passed me."

He recalled those incredibly sexy eyes that she gave back to him after she saw her cards. Even though it cost him the game it was so worth it to see that smile with those intentive eyes. He knew that it had to have earned him dating points or heart win over points, and that was the main thing. Alfie now was ready to talk, "About last night, and all that we have been through these last weeks, you are... you know I never thought it was possible but with you it seems that anything is possible. There is something that I want to tell you but I'm just not sure how."

"Alfie, you know that you can tell me anything."

"Well, let me describe it like this. I am all about sports and programming, but let me start with sports. It is very rare, in football it has only happened once, in baseball there are just a few pitchers that have accomplished this."

"I am not sure what you are saying."

"Okay, The 1972 Dolphins did this and they were the first to do anything like this and it has never been equaled. In baseball Don Larsen did this in the 1956 World Series. What's more important about this is the way that their heart felt after they did it. It makes you feel so alive and brings so much happiness and hope."

"So what did the Dolphins do?"

"They were perfect just like you. What I am trying to tell you is that I think that you're perfect. I am in love with everything about you and the feeling that you give me in my heart when we talk and when we're together is unlike anything anything I have ever felt in my life."

"I am not perfect though Alfie, I have my faults."

"What I am saying is that to me you are perfect. To you you might see faults and mistakes but when I see you I see how incredible you are and what a difference you make in my life and in all of the people around you, I think I wish I could always be with you. You have the purest heart and to me that is so priceless."

"I don't know what to say. No one has ever said anything like this to me before." She immediately went for her strap and it went flying to her shoulder which freed her to do this... She leaned over and Alfie got that kiss and it was everything that he had hoped it to be and more.

Chandler and Angie were deep in conversation across the aisle and Chandler said to Alfie, "Way to go, you know y'all might be able to get a room when we land."

During mid kiss Christie looked up and pulled the curtain shut and they were alone. "Now where were we?" Christie said with an expectant look, giving him those same sexy eyes that she had given him the night before, and also during the hearts game, and yes there was an accompanying smile. And that anticipating seductive smile dove right in to where they had left off.

With the curtains shut and Alfie and Christie romancing away,

Chandler got on the subject of Alfie and yes his kissing exploits. "So guess when Alfie got his first kiss?"

"Must tell."

"It was his senior year and he had just got home from prom, it was prom night, and he got on the phone with the girl that he had taken and I heard them talking. He would never tell me about his love life. He said well, you're a pretty good kisser too. And that was my first knowledge that he was even on the diamond."

"Late bloomer, you know that the great romantics always do bloom late. I wonder why that is?"

"He had been in love with many girls before during his early years, but he had never been kissed. For a while I thought he could be an astronaut with all of his daydreaming about his loves. Earth to Alfred."

"That's sweet, you know I really think that they have something good going."

Across the aisle Christie said, "Oh, Alfie!"

"Yeah, it sure sounds like it." Chandler remarked as he heard her spark a few seats over.

Angie kept the conversation going, "He is so sweet to her, we went shopping at the mall last night and all he could talk about was Christie. How she has the best sense of humor."

Christie let out a giggle and said, "Alfie, you devil." In the cutest way of course.

Angie continued, "He really thinks the world of her."

Chandler had a thought, "By the sounds of it he thinks the Globemaster of her, and he might be joining the mile high club pretty soon."

"They're just kissing."

Behind the curtain Angie and Chandler heard, "Oh goodness Alfie, you're incredible."

"Just kissing? Do those seats lean back?"

Christie them followed it up with, "Ha! That's hilarious."

Chandler felt he had to explain, "Yeah, about that. I always thought that he did inherit the family jewels. Maybe not."

Then Christie laughing her beautiful tail off said, "Oooh."

Chandler responded as he sipped his tea, "Yeah, so I guess its still up in the air."

They could barely hear Alfie talking as he was whispering then they heard Christie say, "Oh goodness Alfie, its enormous."

Chandler smiled, "So...I guess he did."

Christie was enthralled, "Now let me see the other one." There was a pause. "Its's even bigger than the other one."

Angie giggled and said, "So.. I guess it's still up in the air, unless."

Chandler got this expression on his face, "You know, I always thought that they called him The Toro on his baseball team because he was such a good hitter. Could be for other reasons though."

"Hmmm is right. Christie has got some splainin' to do."

The pilots voice came over the loud speaker. "We will be arriving in Sabzwar, Afghanistan at the Shindand Airbase in one hour. Enjoy the rest of your flight."

Angie looked over to Chandler and said with a raised eyebrow, "One hour? Little Alfie could be made in an hour. I better find out what is going on over there."

Chandler was agreeable, "Go for it."

Angie cleared her throat, "Lucy you got some splainin' to do. What on earth are you two doing over there?"

Christie quickly adjusted her collar and got out her compact and proceeded to put on some lipstick and then drew back the curtain. "Nothing."

"My goodness girl you have no idea what it sounds like over here."

Christie thought for a minute and started to Jarrett, cheeks as rouge as they could be, "Oh." She thought some more then her tone went deeper, "Oh. I can explain everything." Then she drew the curtain back further where they could see Alfie. He had his sleeves back to his shoulders and lifted up his left bicep.

Alfie did the splainin', "Laughs and giggles that's all. Why what were you thinking?"

Chandler laughed and Angie noticing his biceps looked over to Chandler and said, "So it is still up in the air."

Chandler summed up their thoughts, "We just didn't know it sounded like you could be in the process of making me a grandad. That's all."

Christie Jarretted even more now they were a deep rose color as she adjusted her blouse. "Can we not kiss in peace? He was just showing me his biceps."

Chandler had a smirk, "Is that all? We thought that you were showing her your..."

Angie cut him off in mid sentence, "Jewelry, Christie does have a nice collection and they are great to compliment and you never know where compliments can get you."

"Speaking of that, you know a grandson would be nice."

"Daaad. All we did was kiss and then I told her some jokes."

Chandler looked like a relived coach after a relief pitcher had just saved the game, "Thank God. Well, we didn't mean to intrude, carry on. Wait a minute, y'all might want to carry on once we get back to the hotel."

Christie closed the curtain and looked over to Alfie with those eyes, bedroom eyes as you could call them and did they ever make him melt. As he was adjusting his sleeve Christie whispered in his ear, "You know you're a great kisser?"

He was now completely adjusted and he turned his head to look over at her and found her lips on his. This was getting good and Alfie was loving every minute of it. Caps were on his mind and not the kind that you wear on your head although that could get interesting with what he had on his mind, no it was the kind of the night.

They were really breathing heavy now and Alfred had to say something, something to really cement their potential together, "Am I the only one that you kiss this way beautiful?"

"What? Of course sexy, there are no other men in my life right now and that is the way that I like it."

"So what would you say to...I don't know, maybe seeing me tonight at the hotel?"

"What would you say to keeping it simple until we get back to New York?" She batted her eyes, those seductive eyes, but right now those eyes were telling him yes while she was saying wait a few days.

Alfie drew back his head, but all he could see were those eyes, "Your eyes are so...so..."

Christie decided to fill in the blank and responded with a perky, "Sexy?"

"Yeah, I don't think that I could ever say no to those eyes, my goodness I melt every time I see you looking at me."

"So you're okay with waiting until we get back?"

"How could I say no? I have waited my whole life for you, what is another few days?"

"Good, it will be hard for me too, so you know. I just want for it to be special and what did Aggie say? Sabzwar, Afghanistan? Well, it's not Paris. And to make you feel better there is a great view of the city from my bedroom window."

"Now that sounds romantic. We could sit at those tables in the back at

Traccia's, candle lit, exotic port with some portibello pasta. You and I and a great conversation and some laughs, is that romantic enough for you?"

"That's more like it, and then we could just go from there and if you have been blessed by God enough it could lead up to my apartment and a nice movie with a view."

"I have been blessed by God by just knowing you, I am so blessed to be with you now. God's blessings go wherever you go."

The pilots voice came over the loud speakers again, "We will be landing shortly, fasten your seat belts."

Aggie and General Watson pulled back the curtain behind them and Aggie said to Alfie and Christie, "We have news that the A-10 Thunderbolts just dropped the netrosia inside the cave complex. I hope you will be accompanying us to the site tomorrow to get you input."

"That's great, and yes we will be. Christie?"

"Sure, I'll go." She said with sparkling eyes.

Aggie lifted up his Apple Ipad, "Here is the first wave."

It was video of the jets launching the missiles into an opening at the base of a mountain. The missile disappeared then a few minutes later there was an Al-Qaeda rebel running out of the opening clasping his throat.

Chapter 14

HINDUKUSH MOUNTAINS

The rebel came running out trying to scream but nothing came out, he was suffocating. Tapesh and his crew had just arrived on the scene and were out of their truck. The gasping man ran up to Tapesh and clawed at his shirt then fell to the ground getting dirt in his mouth. With his last breath that he could muster he said faintly, "They're all dead."

TiHusha obviously didn't like the sound of this, "We have to get out of here they will be here soon to access their impact."

Tapesh nodded at the rest of them and said, "Let's go. We have to get back to the town."

They all loaded up and took off with Tapesh driving, leaving their beloved base in the dust. This was heavy stuff for these men and they didn't want to think about what had just happened, their survival was the only thing on their mind. Tapesh floored it not saying a word, his wife was the only thing on his mind and it seemed to be the same for the rest of the rebels.

Karush was in the back of the truck wincing his eyes with every bump hit, it was a caleche road that had many potholes that weren't agreeing with his stomach. "God I am hungry." He said to Tihusha grabbing his stomach, "You know the last time I ate a steak?"

"I don't want to think about food right now. Did you see how that guy died right in front of us?"

"It was with my wife, we had just been hunting at someone's ranch and they only had a few cows. I only had an AK and well, I got it in the head. She cooked it and it was the best steak I have ever eaten."

"He just died, right there, we all saw the missiles go in. What the heck was that stuff?"

"It was grilled perfect, medium well. She also made some mashed potatoes. God I am missing her right now." "Why did he suffocate like that? He was right there out in the open air and he just couldn't breathe. Muzza is gone Karush." He paid him no attention and was more concerned about his stomach.

The transport truck rattled and hummed scurrying across the dusty caleche road. Tapesh had it floored and they were about 16 miles away from the base and 9 miles away from their town. There was a curve straight ahead and when he made the turn a US Army transport truck passed them going about 40 miles an hour. After the curve he put the pedal to the metal, not knowing if there were more on the way or if they would turn around.

A few miles down the road another US Army passed the guys in a rush. Tapesh was giving it all he could and the truck couldn't go any faster in the condition that the road was in. Tapesh was praying that they would not turn around. If they did they could all be killed as the Army soldiers had better weapons and more trucks than the rebels. This could be disastrous if they were to turn around or even worse if they had a roadblock setup in front of them. But, they were almost to the town of Charikar where their wives would be so happy to see them alive.

The brownish white dust of the caleche had began to dissipate behind them and just when it cleared Tapesh and the guys in the back noticed the first Army truck that had passed them. Now they were six miles away from their home town and approaching fast, but even faster the Army truck was closing in on them. The rebels in the back went straight for their AK's and proceeded to shoot at the truck thinking they could blow out a tire. They fired many shots in their direction and got a good solid hit on the left side windshield.

As the Army truck approached they could see blood splattered on the left side windshield, it didn't stop them though. Karush yelled out in his Afghan accent, "The tires, shoot for the tires. They are getting closer."

While a few of them were reloading an Army soldier popped out of the left side window and got off a few shots. Ricochet's rang out inside the awning of the back of the coyote brown rebel truck. One of the bullets deflected from the iron awning and hit Tihusha in the leg, he kept of firing at the tire and with one quick pull of the trigger an onslaught of bullets spurt out directly at their front right tire.

It was a blowout, "Victory!" Proclaimed Tihusha as he set his gun aside and tended to his wound. The Army truck took a quick turn to the right and with their speed they saw the truck flip several times before it came to a halt, dust and dirt arose in a gigantic cloud. As soon as the truck had stopped the other Army truck came flying around the side of it taking out some mesquites puncturing their left tire. They were leaking air but, speeding right at them even faster then the first.

Tihusha was wounded, and by the looks of it, it was pretty bad. It was in his leg though and he could still hold a rifle and bare the pain with every shot that was required of him. So in a tough grimace Tihusha brought his rifle into aim and began to fire again at their tires. Tapesh noticed the first signs of civilization as they passed a farm on their right, it was a quick blur though. They were getting close to the turnoff street and he was so ready to get rid of these guys.

Quietly Tihusha took aim and said to himself, "One more and we're free. You can do this." He squeezed the trigger and blasted their left tire. The Army truck went toppling in a heap of dust. Karush hugged Tihusha and said, "You did it my friend. Are you okay?"

Tihusha kind of laughed it off and said, "Just a flesh wound, my spirit is free."

Karush ripped off his sleeve and wrapped it around his wound as Tihusha winced in pain. Karush exclaimed, "We will get you better in no time my friend."

"Thank you, you are the best." Tihusha said moving his rifle to the side with his knee as the back was cramped for space.

Tapesh made the turn at their street and they all went to their homes. The US Army searched for them later on that day but they had already escaped. After a few days they relinquished their positions in the rebel army. Tapesh went on to be an erect underwear model in Europe, his wife said he had great potential. Tihusha now is a stripper pole salesman in France. Karush is a pro football cheerleader scout for the Miami Dolphins.

Chapter 15

Hilton Hotel Sabzwar, Afghanistan

All of the crew was gathered in Aggie's presidential suite at the Hilton in Sabzwar, Afghanistan. Angie had one of the room's exquisite decorations, a golden detailed elephant, in her hand and was asking Chandler about it. Alfie and Christie were out on the balcony holding hands and talking to their hearts content. They looked like they could be on their honeymoon by the romantic glances Christie was giving Alfie. Alfie was telling her a story, "Did you know that I met Usain St. Leo Bolt?"

"I am Catholic but I don't know that much about the Saints. Who is that?" Christie asked with the cutest smile knowing he was going to tell her all about him.

"You know the famous Olympian winner of the 100m and 200m dash at the Beijing Olympics in 08'."

"Oh that Usain Bolt. Surely you can't be serious. You met him? Was it an H&G?"

"Yes, I am serious and don't call me Shirley."

"I would think that he would be so fast that you wouldn't even remember meeting him. Shake hands, gone in a flash."

"Well, we didn't discuss Olympic politics or anything and now that I think about it, it was pretty fast. It was in the lobby of his hotel and there were tons of people around him. It was a few days before he competed. I remember the night before I was so hungover I did keg stands till morning. Then he ran away with the gold."

"That is a really interesting story, I am just glad we're not that fast or at least I am not. I like to take things slow watch the passion simmer."

"Really? I am so slow then it could take me an hour to run around the track once, and that's without taking breaks."

"You know though, bolting isn't always that bad though."

"Tell me more."

"Well, let's just say that if we were Romeo and Juliet I would bolt off with you in a minute, say via con dios to the parents and elope in a heartbeat. Probably faster than Usain St. Leo."

"Is that a fact? I need to go talk to my dad for a minute."

"And what about?"

"Nothing."

"Tell me." Her head was down and she looked up at him with those sparkling brown eyes.

"I can't say no to those eyes, its not fair. Okay, I was just going to see just how fast you really are."

"How do you figure?"

"Well if he opposed our getting married then there might be a chance of you bolting."

"Oh, Romeo."

"Would it work?"

"Well, you see the story goes that they were in love and as for us...I don't know."

"Yeah, I guess you have to fall in love first. I guess we will just have to wait and see if we fall."

"I am definitely leaning...we'll see..." She said batting her eyes. "I'm not saying its impossible, with you there seems to be nothing that is impossible for you. And if you just applied that kind of know how to our romance... well I would have to say that there would be nothing that you, we couldn't accomplish."

General Watson was showing Aggie some new videos on his laptop at the oversized presidential desk in the lavish living room. Aggie said, "Are we ready?"

"Sure, gather them around."

Aggie went over to where Angie and Chandler were and said, "We are ready if y'all have a minute."

"Sure, be right there."

Once they were all gathered around the desk General Watson began to talk, "Congratulations to all of you on the project it was a phenomenal success. If you haven't seen this already it is a video of the A-10 Thunderbolts launching the netrosia missile into the Hindukush mountain complex. As of now we are unsure of how many casualties the missile claimed, however we do know that most of the rebels that were in the complex were killed. We are now awaiting a presidential address concerning the outcome of the event."

The General clicked over to Fox News and the president Barak Obama was at the podium about to deliver a speech. They all watched as the suspense grew. The President said, "Thank you all for coming on such short notice. As you may know we have been at war with Al-Qaeda for some time now. Today at 1:04 PM our Air Force launched a new anti-terrorist missile that was designed to destroy all inhabitants of the cave complex in the Hindukush mountains of Afghanistan, where Al-Qaeda's central base was supposed to be."

Barak looked up from the page and continued, "Soldiers at our Army base near those mountains have combed the cave complex and found over 40 bodies and it is with my great pleasure to announce to you that at approximately 4:13 PM one of our soldiers found and identified the body of the leader of the terrorist organization Osama Bin Laden. All of the Al-Qaeda rebels including Osama died of asphyxiation. This is a significant victory for the United States and our war on terror. We hope that with the help of God that this will serve to be an essential stepping stone to ending this war that has cost the lives of numerous Americans."

General Watson let out a, "Whoop!" He was an Aggie.

All of them began hugging each other in their excitement. Alfie said to Christie, "You did it!"

"We did it. All of us worked together on this."

"You're right. Dad way to go."

"I'm proud of you son."

"Thanks Dad, since you're so proud of me I guess you'll be buying our dinner tonight."

"I guess I could, but first someone order some champagne."

In a few minutes they all had glasses of champagne poured and General Watson was ready to give a toast. "First, a toast to all of the men and women who lost their lives in the terrorist attacks. And to all of our soldiers that have died fighting this war on terror."

"Here, here."

Their crystal glasses clanked and their pinkies were held high as they all took a gulp of champagne. "And now a toast to all of you whose hard work made all of this possible. We couldn't have done it without you."

"Cheers!"

They drank proudly with their pinkies in the air and mingled with stories for a while then it was back to business. General Watson received a call and then spoke to the crew, "I would like to invite all of you to join Aggie and I in going on site tomorrow at the Hindukush mountains. Just so you know all of the dead bodies will have been removed by then. We would just like for you to help us find out any more information that you can about their facilities."

They all agreed and then they were off to the lobby and to wait on the bus to get there. Once it arrived they all piled into this yellow short bus and took their seats. Alfie and Christie sat next to each other right behind the bus driver. The bus driver was very energetic and wore a colorful turban. Once they were all inside he asked in an Afghan accent, "Oh my friend it is such a beautiful day, where am I taking you to? I will drive you anywhere you want to go to, all free service, I am a very cheap date I'm free."

Alfie had talked to the desk clerk and she recommended that they go to a nearby local place so Alfie said, "Larsa Sports Bar."

In his distinct voice the bus driver said, "Very good choice you will love their Goats and rooster eggs. And off we go."

The driver pressed down and gave it the gas and he let out a toot, the bus did not move. "Oh goodness my stomach, I ate way too much curry chicken for lunch."

Alfie was doing his best not to laugh, "Where do you go for gas? I am sorry we didn't get your name."

"The name is Edwasa and I always go to Terran Coit."

"Do they have what is it called anti..."

"Terrorist's weapons?"

"No, you know Gas-x or what is it called...Bean..."

"Oh that smells like roses." Edwasa finished the sentence again.

"Goodness what kind of roses do you grow here?"

"No that is the name of the medicine, Bean, Oh that smells like roses. No actually that smells like crude oil or Cow methane."

"Yeah I would say so, why don't we go get some of that first."

"There are not any cows for miles and the oil fields are far away."

"No, just go to Terran Coit you know the gas station to get some of that Bean, Oh that smells like roses."

"Oh good because if you wanted Cow methane we would have to wait for them to toot and that could take hours, but it would be worth it."

"Gross, lets just go to Terran Coit."

"Ok, great idea, we go." Edwasa gave it the gas and this time the engine was turned on and they were off and running.

Terran Coit was quite a gas station, there was no wonder that it was the world's largest oil company. Edwasa was in and out in no time flat. He came back to his seat with a bag and all of it was in the bag so he popped his pills and washed them down with a Terran Cola. Then they were off to the Larsa Sports Bar and about halfway there Alfie noticed the smell of roses and asked Christie, "That is the most lovely perfume what is it called?"

"Degree for women, I didn't put on any perfume today."

"Is it rose fragrant Degree?"

"Tropical melon."

"What is that smell did he buy some roses for his woman or something?"

"I don't know but I smell it too, ask him."

"Edwasa, did you buy roses?"

"Yes can you smell them?"

"Yeah, they smell great."

Edwasa ever so slightly lifted his left leg, Alfie didn't notice but, "There it is again, a strong odor of roses."

They were a block away from the Bar and Edwasa was surveying the parking situation, "The bar is really packed tonight." There were cars everywhere and for a while there it looked like there were no parking spots. A parking spot opened up then a small Ford Fiesta pulled in and Edwasa gunned it to pull in before but the Fiesta was too fast.

On the Fiesta's bumper it said,

"Honk if you love Jesus!

Text and drive if you want to see him."

Then out of no where a dusty green Saab pulled out of a spot right in front of the bar. "Victory, we have found a parking spot."

Alfie jokingly said, "My Jetta could barely fit in that space."

"Don't worry my friend I am a pro at this." Keep in mind that they were in a bus that was kind of wide, much wider than a car and much longer too. "I will fit us in there like a glove."

"Maybe, if it was a woman's glove with Arnold Swartznegger's hand."

"Watch and learn grasshopper." Edwasa drove all the way up to the point to where he made the turn and then he kept on turning the huge steering wheel and slowly the bus made it closer to the parking block. Then the right side of the bus looked like it was going to hit the back left bumper of the car on the right. Edwasa straightened it out then scooted it in there and it was a perfect fit, not an inch to spare on each side.

How in the world did he not graze the cars on either side? It was a miracle. Alfie was amazed so he stood up and said to all that were in the bus, "He parked this bus in here like it was a car." He ran the center aisle of the bus and looked on both sides in amazement as did the other passengers.

When they had all fully understood what Edwasa had just done they all burst out laughing. In all of the laughing Aggie wanted to know, "How are we getting out of here?"

Edwasa had an answer, "I will open the back door and we will all just get out that way."

The short Afghan guy unlatched the back door, emergency door, and they all piled out with the General and Alfie helping the ladies out to the asphault parking lot. When Alfie helped Christie they never let go and held hands all the way up to the Bar entrance. It appeared that there was some sort of wait to get into the bar so they formed a close line with Edwasa standing directly in front of Alfie and Christie and would they be in for a treat.

Edwasa felt one coming on in his stomach then it proceeded down the intestinal highway, he was on the verge, he looks over both shoulders then tries to silently let it go. And he did, Alfie caught a wiff and noticed the flowers to his side and thought, goodness there that smell is again, quite refreshing. The country air was so refreshing he had to say something so he did, "That is the most lovely smell and this time I think it is the flowers."

Christie said, "Yes those are quite lovely flowers and what a beautiful smell."

Edwasa was just laughing after he heard them talking. He turns around and said, "Actually that is the all natural herbal blend of exotic flowers."

"Yes, they are so fragrant."

"No, it is the Bean, Oh that smells like roses."

"You mean your gas-x."

"Yes when I go tootie toot it makes it smell like roses. Over here in Afghanistan we don't know how to git rid of gas so we just make it smell better."

"Hence, the roses."

"Yes, the roses."

Alfie was now recalling when he had been smelling that same smell and he now came to understand that it was from Edwasa's..., "Gross, that is disgusting. How did they do that? It smells just like roses."

"I know that is the great part, no cologne just gas."

"Goodness I need a drink."

"They have this great rose cocktail..."

"No more roses."

There was a very large woman, about 400lbs in front of a man and his son in the line ahead of Alfie and Christie. The lady looked to be out of breath and was shifting her weight on the wooden bridge entrance-way and it made the whole bridge shift. So Alfie started watching this woman then something started flashing from her transparent purse and it made loud beeps. The boy grabbed onto his Dad, and then very scared with no place to go said, "It's backing up!" The boy was scared out of his mind envisioning a tractor or a large truck backing up and running over him, and started screaming. "Save me Daddy!"

Alfie and Christie burst out laughing as the large woman answered her cell phone. Then a large group just left the building and passed by them and they went in and found a table. Chandler noticed the large bosomed local lady in the green dress at the main bar as they walked by. He decided that he would go and talk to her but not now. The menus were bilingual and offered many drinks and appealing appetizers then Alfie saw it, the Rose Bloom. Uhh, no thanks.

Edwasa thought he would be the funny guy and order it so he did when the girl next door waitress came to the table. The lady in the green dress got up and Chandler thought that she was leaving but she made a turn just before she got to the front and went to the restroom. The guy that was doing his best to play his cards right left so this gave Chandler the clue to go and snag her up before some other sleezebag did.

Chandler loved his conversations with Angie but he could tell that she preferred Italians so he thought that he had a better chance with the mystery woman at the bar. He took the guys seat at the bar and when she came back from the restroom she found a drink waiting for her then Chandler went to work.

"The world needs more beautiful women like you in it. It would make my job a lot easier."

"So you work for an organization where their main priority is finding talented beautiful women. Is this an interview?"

"Depends on what your talents are?"

"I thought that my eyes or lipstick would speak for themselves, and if that wasn't enough this dress should do."

"Those are the best talents to have."

"But is it what you're looking for?"

"Well I'm certainly not going to make you take any I.Q tests."

"What if I don't want the job?"

"Right, I guess I should tell you more about it." And he did as the rest of the guys were ordering their meals back at the table. There were chips on the table and Alfie was indulging himself with his Afghan local beer. Christie had a white wine and a few chips for herself whenever Alfie wasn't in the bowl. All Alfie could think about was their date that they would go on when they got back to New York.

"You must tell me Angie what would you recommend on the menu at Traccia's?"

"Traccia's what about Michael Jordan's Steakhouse?

"We can go there next time, Angie told me about their new addition for romance. Sounds interesting."

"Well, there is the lasagna which is outstanding, can't go wrong with the lasagna."

"I was wondering if it had any mushrooms in the lasagna?"

"Yes and several kinds."

"Delightful, then I shall have it. And for you my dear?" Alfie gave Christie that look.

"I am not sure yet, there is so much to choose from, anything will be great as long as it includes a conversation with you. I am not half as concerned with the food as I am in getting to know you better Alfie."

"And I you, and I aim to please."

"You don't have to do anything special Alfie, just be you."

"I know I can be entertaining if you want for me to be, if you want to laugh I'll just watch a few Seinfeld shows before the date and everything will work out."

"I am sure it would, you're funny without telling any jokes, but I do love Jerry, he is hilarious."

"Dating these days is always so awkward and uncertain, but we have this head start on the first one."

"On first dates I wish we could just wear signs."

"Just signs?"

"Well you know clothes and a sign."

"Aww, I was really hoping that the sign would be really small. You are quite gorgeous you know."

"No, you know signs."

"Okay what would yours say?"

"Well... if I were on a date with you it would say, yes."

"Wait, I saw that somewhere, was that in one of Kevin Costner's movies?"

"For the love of the game, but it is a good idea."

"And it would say yes, goodness I wish we were on the date right now, you know mine would be a question like one word, sex with a question mark."

"Hey, that wasn't what I was saying yes to."

"Oh, why not? Am I not good looking enough for you?"

"There is so much more to this chastity belt than that."

"Isn't that from another Kevin Costner movie, Prince of Thieves?"

"Close, its of the spoof, Men in Tights."

"Well I think that the key to unlocking maid Marian's chastity belt was just saving her. And I've already done that a few times."

"Alfie, I can't believe we're talking about this goodness where is the romance?"

"Sorry, I guess I was getting ahead of myself there."

"Way ahead, there is much to be romanced before we even talk about unlocking chastity belts."

"You're right, I am a guy, and you're soooo..."

"So what?"

"Beautiful and did I say perfect."

"If I am perfect for you then you should be concentrating on the long term and not just the passion in your loins that is temporary."

"Unless you gain about 400 pounds there will always be passion in these loins for you my maid."

"You are such a guy."

"I know."

"But I like you even if you are a guy."

"Thank God, I wasn't looking forward to a sex change operation if that's what it would take to get you. You know I would do anything to get you."

"In bed? Yes, I can see that."

"No, get you and never let you go."

"Okay, now that was romantic. More of that will get you where you want to be."

"Where I want to be is to hear our rings click when we hold hands dancing."

"Well there is a ton of romance between now and that point so I would just take it one rose at a time."

"Edwasa do you have anymore of the rose fragrance?"

"Yeah here's the pack."

"Right here I have enough rose power to get us married tonight."

"Alfie that is disgusting."

Their food arrived and the cheeseburger that Alfie ordered looked incredible so he dug in.

Christie had to specify herself, "Real roses Aflie, and at the rate you're going you're going to need a ton of them."

"It was just a joke."

"You better make it up to me and show me that you're serious about us. And our relationship isn't just dust in the wind."

"I have known you just a few weeks and I can safely say that you are such an amazing person that every moment since I have known you, you have occupied my every thought not all of them, but I just have this heart for you and my heart has changed, my attitude has changed and when I get around you, when it's just us, I become this person that I always dreamed that I would be."

"The dust is beginning to dissipate but I still smell roses."

Edwasa said with a grin, "Opps, yeah I couldn't hold it back, its that curry, goodness its potent."

Alfie had to laugh then he got serious. "Okay, did you know that there a millions of Emperor Penguins?"

"Alfie I can still smell it. The air is thick."

"No really, I am getting to it, a male Emperor penguin will search for years throughout the Arctic through the millions of penguins and when he finds the one, I mean the right one for him, he stays with her for the rest of his life. They all look the same, it is amazing how he can tell her apart from all the other female penguins, but he does, he memorizes everything about her, the one and when he goes to get food and comes back to look for her he knows exactly what to look for because he has memorized everything that makes her unique from all the other penguins. Out of all the other women that I have ever met there has never been anyone that is as funny, sophisticated, witty, and unique as you. And now that I have found you when I go to the store and see some hottie, I don't blink because I have already found the one, and I will always come back to your loving arms."

They were sitting right next to each other and after Christie heard that and got a little misty eyed she held her arms out and embraced Alfie in a passionate hug. Alfie pulled back and looked into those incredible eyes and said softly, "All my life, I have been searching, and I have already found you. I will never let you go."

"I don't know what to say, but I am thankful that I too have found you. I just don't want to be left standing in the rain."

"Christie, if I ever left you standing in the rain it would be to get us an umbrella."

Angie was starting to cry and went for the napkins. Edwasa was very moved too, "Goodness y'all are so perfect for each other."

Christie and Alfie were holding hands underneath the table and just looking at each other. Christie said, "I think we're going to get a taxi back to the hotel."

Alfie smiled and nodded, "Yeah, I think we have some more talking to do tonight." He looks over to her, "Maybe under the stars on the balcony?"

"Yes, I would like that."

They were gone in a minute and on their way out they expected to tell Chandler that they were leaving but when they got there, Chandler and the woman in the green dress were already gone.

In the taxi there was a bollywood song playing on the radio from a movie that they had never seen, but the way that their night was going it could be dramatized by a singing and dancing love story with a happy ending. And for a while in the taxi, Christie, the romantic that she is could just see themselves breaking out into songs with dots on their foreheads both ecstatic as they can be, declaring their love for each other. And even though Christie would never, at this point, two weeks in, way too early, say that she loved him. He could see it in her eyes when they talked though and knew it by the way that she talked to him.

There was a dating rule that if you ever wanted something serious in the future that you should never, two weeks into a relationship, tell the other person that you love them, you just didn't do it. They were so infatuated with each other though they did show it in what they would do for each other though.

Once they arrived at the Hilton they were greeted by the staff and in the lobby Alfie saw a bouquet of flowers in a gift shop that he went over an bought. Christie waited at the front desk and when Alfie walked up to her with a basket full of flowers he looked down at them, then up into her eyes and said, "These are for you."

Her heart melted, "You came back to me."

"I always will." He handed the flowers to her.

"They're beautiful! Thank you Alfie you're the best."

"Your exquisite beauty was on my mind when I saw them and knew that they should belong to you, the best bio-chemist in the world."

"The best programmer in the world sure does know how to give great compliments and make my heart melt."

"If everything goes according to plans there is still more heart melting to be felt in the day so shall we?" Alfie extends his arm towards the elevator.

"We shall." Christie nods with a smile of anticipation.

On the way to the elevator she noticed that there was on rose in the bunch of flowers and thought that Alfie must be listening to her. "Look Alfie a rose, you know that the best way to take things in a relationship is one rose at a time. This is the first."

"This is the first orgainc rose..." Alfie pressed the floor that they were going to. "The first was the silk rose in which I saved your life. The second rose was on my phone after I saved you the second time and you saved mine right back. This is the first rose that was grown on a bush, organic."

"The best things in life are organic."

"I agree if you are talking about the way your hotel room shampoo makes the women on the commercial feel."

"Commercial?"

"Herbal Essences the organic shampoo?"

"Right, but there are so many organic things being made today that once were never possible, gasoline from algae, motor oil from corn, netrosia had some organic elements in it. Hybrid, really, we had to synthesize part of the compound."

They were at their floor and being the debonair gentleman that he was he motioned for her to go out first. "After you."

"Thank you."

"Tennis is going organic."

Not sure what he was talking about, "Do you mean that in an Herbal Essences commercial way?"

"No, but now that you have mentioned it those female tennis players really do make some serious noises out there. If I am in the other room I don't know if it's When Harry met Sally or whether the remote changed over to the playboy channel. No I was talking about the balls and rubbers."

"Rubbers and balls?"

"Yeah you know the tennis balls are now being made of hemp and organic rubbers."

Christie burst out laughing and caught her breath, "Oh my goodness, I wasn't sure what you were talking about there for a minute. For a minute there I had thought that you had gone left side democrat on me there."

"Still an elephant, as conservative as George Bush."

They were at her room, "I am just going to go in and freshen up for a minute I'll be over to your room in a bit."

"Okay...I'll just be..." She shut the door and he reluctantly went to his room and lit the candles and took them out to the luxurious balcony. In a hurry he went back in the room and took the champagne off ice and set it on the table on the balcony. His goal was to let her see just how romantic he could be without saying how much in love with her that he was. Note to self don't say the word love. There, hopefully it would wouldn't come out of his mouth, she would freak.

Def Leppard began to play on his phone, pour some sugar on me, he answered it, "Hello."

"I am outside."

"Be right there."

He walked over towards the door and opened it, she had changed into this extremely sexy dress that came up just above mid thigh. It had two straps and no back, it was dark blue and almost satiny feel to it when he hugged her.

"My goodness, you get more gorgeous every time I see you, come in. I hope you weren't out there too long."

"Long enough."

"I am so sorry I was just getting everything ready."

"No, long enough to see your Dad."

"My Dad? What was he doing?"

"He said hello, then slipped into his room with the woman in the green dress."

"Why did I even ask I should have known. Anyway lets go out to the balcony and have some champagne."

"Just a few sips, I am already kinda tipsy."

They sat down in the chairs and had a view that overlooked the city. Christie said, "It's beautiful."

Alfie had his eyes on Christie and said, "It most certainly is, the most beautiful thing I have ever seen."

"Goodness if you like this city you should see Paris."

He was still looking directly at her, "This one has captured my heart."

"We have only been here a day."

"And yet it feels like I have known it my whole life, I just want to get to know it better. So tell me, to you what is critical to making a relationship work?"

She looked up at the stars that were out in full effect, "Many things really, communication and knowing what you want out of it. If I know what you want then it is so much easier to please you. If I don't I might as well be kissing the wind."

"I once heard someone say that every relationship gets to the point where one wants out for whatever reason and you have to make a decision. You can either tear up the perfect picture that you have in your mind of the other person and accept them for who they are or...You can tear down the person and end the relationship. If we ever get to that point I hope that I have shown you enough love that you will know how much you mean to me and that you will realize that I'm not perfect and that we all make mistakes."

"I don't think that it would ever get to that with us, but if it did I hope I would make the right decision."

"No matter where our relationship goes there is always room to grow and room to build. I am a builder as if you haven't noticed I love to just build you up to make you better than you ever were if that is possible. With you, you were perfect to begin with. I will always give you my undivided attention and constant appreciation."

Christie was just looking up at the stars that were gleaming in the distant night sky. Her eyes were in the heavens but her heart was sitting next to her. Alfie noticed this and asked, "What are you looking at...I mean do you know much about the stars?"

"Just thinking."

The conversation had taken her to an entirely different place so Alife thought that he should speak and he did, "Did you know that I actually learned something in college?"

"Obviously you are a successful programmer I am sure that you learned a lot."

"Actually its about stars."

"Oh? Do tell."

"One of Newton's laws of Physics is that to every action there is an equal and opposite reaction."

"Does this have to do with dating?"

"I guess it could it would be so unfair though."

"How's that?"

"Well if my action is to ask you if I could kiss you and there was an equal and OPPOSITE reaction then I would get slapped."

"Yeah that could hurt."

"But, if you look at it like this, if two heavenly bodies were to collide, and I think that your body is so heavenly."

"Really?"

"Yes, out of this world, anyway if two heavenly bodies collide then the equal and opposite reaction would be that it would rock both worlds."

"UUHHum!" Christie cleared her throat after hearing that.

"...So to speak." Alfie did his best to correct the situation.

Being the witty gal that she is Christie said, "So Benjamin Braddock are you wanting to rock my world?" Very seductively Christie gave him the bedroom eyes.

"Well Mrs. Robinson." Taken back by the question he didn't know what to say.

"Answer the question Benjamin." Stern in her response she demanded something of him.

"Yes...that would be a yes. Wait up... Are you trying to seduce me Mrs. Robinson?" Alfie totally played the part then they both started laughing.

"I love that movie." Christie said as she took a sip of champagne.

"I love that about you."

"What?"

"That we can joke around about anything. Nothing's sacred."

"Nothing?"

"Well of course the holy grail." Alfie lifted up his glass.

"The holy grail, yes, just a flesh wound."

"Did you know that I didn't even know what the holy grail was until I saw it about a year ago. I never got it until then."

"Good for you. A toast then...to the quest for the holy grail."

"The quest." They clanged glasses and drank bottoms up. "The best scene is when Sir Galahad goes to the castle of Anthrax with all of those women who do everything they can to seduce him. They take off his belt to examine him and he gets up to leave. Then the other knigits go and get him and he never wants to leave."

"Monty Python such great humor. Did you know that when I was in College I worked for WPG a surveying company?"

"No, I guess I didn't know that."

"Yes, and I got the idea for my own business I wanted to call it third leg surveyors. Catchy isn't it?"

"The tripod thing, third leg I get it."

"I started the business nothing formal at all, just a female sports reporter."

"And how has business been?"

"Booming."

"You are so hilarious. Well you gotta know where to build."

"Precisely. You in the mood for a game of football? I could be the only female sports reporter in the locker room."

"That does sound intriguing. You be the center and I'll be the quarterback and for the first day we can just work on snapping the ball."

"Who needs a ball?"

"Don Larsen."

"Yeah give him the ball and we can practice. He could also be the cameraman."

"You're perfect, we can joke around about anything and I just love that about you."

"Why thank you, sentiments are mutual. You know when I am with you there is no shadow from me."

"Wheew, over my head, explain." Alfie passsed his hand over his head.

"Think about it. Does a light bulb make a shadow?"

"Only if its not turned on."

"No shadow."

"Running with that thought, there are these deep sea creatures that emit light to communicate with the other sea creatures. What if when we got turned on your breasts lit up or my pants began to glow?"

"Okay, that is hilarious. No shadow."

"Precisely." Christie was getting those bedroom eyes for real this time, looking over at Alfie. She then looked back to the room and asked, "Do you want to go watch TV?"

"Yeah, maybe the Graduate is on, or the Quest for the Holy Grail."

"Yeah, I don't think that we would need a TV for that one, its already begun."

Alfie backed up his chair and stood up and went over and took Christie's hand and when she stood up they embraced with a warm, wet kiss. They then took it into the bedroom and when Alife laid her out on the bed she hit the TV power button and the TV turned on.

They were passionately kissing and thoughts were going through Christie's head that she so much wanted for this to happen. As for Alfie she had him at the words, "Rock my world." Alife was thinking, "Okay, I have perfection right here and we're kissing and everything has been going great so I think this is going to happen tonight."

Just as Alfie was thinking that Angie walked in and said, "Oh, goodness, I am sorry I can come back later." They still had on their clothes.

Christie pulled back reluctantly and began to re-access the situation and then she decided that it would be best if they just called it a night. "Alfie I am sorry, but we can pick up right where we left off with a real date tomorrow night in New York."

Great I was so close, "Yeah, that sounds great."

"Angie, don't leave I want to talk to you." Christie leaped up and adjusted her dress then went to catch up with Angie.

Chapter 16

KUDESH, HINDUKUSH MOUNTAINS 8:00AM

Streams of light began to crest over the mountaintops glistening with snow from the night before. It was daybreak and the crew was already to the Al-Qaeda Kudesh base where the air was filled with the scent of sage that imbued their nostrils, as they took in the fresh air. General Watson headed up the mission and after they had exited the transport vehicle they were at the same entrance that Muzza had crawled out from to his death one day before.

They knew nothing of the plight of the rebels, they were there for one reason only as General Watson detailed, "We are here to gather data that could be useful to getting information about where the other rebel bases could be. We know that this is only the start of defeating this vigilant underground uprising of the Al-Qaeda force. We know that this is just part of a much larger network of rebels and if you find anything, log it in your report and gather materials to be analyzed by the CIA. All reports will be given to Kerry Carpenter of the anti-terrorist division of the CIA. Any questions about something just ask myself or Aggie here. Lets get started. Aggie and I will be in the communication room, Alfie and Christie will go to the office of Tapesh, and Angie and Chandler will be in the ammo room. Let's go."

All the dead guys were removed the day before so they had a fresh start and on the ground there was a green powder where the netrosia had settled in. There were lights above as they walked through descending in the cave, to their designated rooms. Angie was wondering about what happened with Chandler last night so she decided to pry, "Do you think this mission will be as successful as your mission was last night?"

"I wasn't on a mission last night."

"What would you call it then? You left me there with Edwasa after Christie and Alfie left."

"It was more of a recruitment."

"Into what the Chandler Army Navy exchange? Well I hope you wore a helmet and the seamen stayed on board."

"She was hired only for some temporary undercover work though."

"How despicable, you are a pig. A one night stand?"

"What did you expect? A trip to Vegas and us married with an ordained Elvis then a house in the suburbs and a family of 8 children?"

"No, but I expected more out of you, that's all."

"Do you like James Bond movies?"

"Yeah."

"What do you expect out of him?"

"Some good action."

"And what does that include?"

"Okay, okay, I see where this is going, but still."

"I don't get nearly as much action as Bond."

"Yeah, but his movies only come out once every two years."

"Okay, so I do actually get more action than him, but still."

"But still what? You're still a pig."

"I am a guy and when I see a beautiful woman my instincts take over, it's the same with you and other hot men."

"I don't go after them for one night stands."

"Men are wired differently than women, women have a longer attention span and think long term, well most of them. So what kind of woman are you? Or are you mad at me because you liked me?"

"I like you, but after that, no way. I am the Vegas, Elvis, suburb, family type. Long term, no ADD."

"I was that type when Alfie's mom and I were together, but she hurt me too many times and I lost respect for the average woman and now I just use them like she used me. Only I am a gentleman and I get the Bond girl almost whenever I want. Is that so wrong? Long term just leads to deep hurts."

"Not if it's the right woman."

"She was so the right woman, but she changed, she morphed into this evil villain, it's better to stay away from anything that looks long term."

"My parents are still together after 40 years and my mom never turned into an evil villain, you just have to find the right one that will always come back to you."

"She always came back alright, just to lash out more hurt, no thanks."

"There is a woman out there that is the Vegas, Elvis, suburb, family type that could love you."

"Well I haven't found her yet, and I'm not looking. I take life one night stand at a time."

They had made it to the ammo room at least that's what the map said, so they opened the door to find some other CIA agents rummaging around. One of the CIA agents, dressed in a formal business skirt suit, looked just like, "Chandler?"

"Rosemary?"

"What are you doing here?"

"What are you doing here?"

"I work for the CIA anti-terrorist division, and you?"

"Air Force, cyberspace programming division."

"And you're here because..."

"I helped my son program the netrosia missile."

"Oh, well congratulations we have to thank you for that."

"Thank you? It was mostly him and Christie that you should thank, I just did some minor repairs."

"All the same."

"I guess we should get to work."

"Right."

The other CIA guys were putting all of the AK's and guns into a crate that was to be taken back to the Army base for analysis. It was a rather large room with several overhead lights, they did have their own lighting system though that was already set up. Chandler went over with Angie into one corner that only had empty crates and thought that they could find some of the shipping destinations as viable data for their mission. It was aparent that all of the AK crates were from Iran and had a destination address that said, "Kudesh Afghanistan."

Chandler was picking up every crate that was in the room and then, after he got to the bottom of the pile, he found a crate that still had something in it. It was a 6 foot cube with packing around one central cylinder and it had a full shipping address on it.

From: General Tapesh

Kudesh Hindukush, Afghanistan
To: AJR
Sasawaha, Somalia

They called out over to the other guys across the room, "Anybody got a crowbar?"

A suit picked one up and brought it over to Chandler. "Here ya go."

"Thanks." Chandler climbed on top of the wooden crate that had some tough nails keeping it together. He picked up the crowbar that he had placed on top and then lodged it in between the top plank, and the side panels, and dug in. After a few whacks at it he had the first one pried up and there were several more to go. The packing was some kind of thick foam that he stood on as he pried up the rest of the planks.

The foam was pretty sturdy and held his weight, after the last one was on the floor he jumped down and dug into the sides. After there was enough room to work with he began tearing into the foam which was like a hot Samurai sword through a Ninja's neck. After a few whacks he hit the payload with a, "Ting," then began tearing away at it with his hands. Angie was just watching and giving suggestions on how he should tear away the foam. He paid no attention and removed a good sum of the top of the encased foam. When he got to the base of the cylinder that was about a foot in diameter he dug his hands in there and yanked the thing out of there.

Chandler said with glee, "It's hollow, just a shell. Imagine that."

Angie had some input, "Maybe, this was supposed to be shipped to Somalia where it would get the nuclear weapon inserted in it?"

"Maybe, I don't know what else would go in it. It certainly is a nuclear casing. Will you help me take this over to our crate?"

"Gladly." A mouse ran across their path as they were making their way over to the crate. The mouse made it into it's hole that was in the base of the wall.

Just then Alfie and Christie walked in through the door with a stack of papers in their hands. "Dad, I can tell you've been doing your job over here. What is it?"

Chandler and Angie set the casing into the crate and Chandler straightened out his back with an arch and a bend then said, "Okay, we found this crate that had shipping tags on it to go to Somalia then I opened the thing up and found this casing for a nuclear weapon. This doesn't look good, there must be another base in Somalia, but where is Sasawaha?"

Alfie responded with some gestures holding out the papers and said,

"We found a ton of paperwork for something they call Harmanja, they said that it translates into bird dropping whatever that is. And there is a ton of paperwork for this Harmanja. Take a look on the casing and see if it says Harmanja anywhere on it."

They all went over to the crate and Chandler turned around the casing and found some Arabic lettering they couldn't decipher. Then as he turned it about 180 he found some small English words that said, "AJR Harmanja America."

"That's it. It is a nuclear weapon." Alfie said with distinction and a proactive air of confidence.

Christie folded her arms and said, "They have to investigate this base in Somalia. Bird droppings could be a missile launched from a jet, a nuclear missile dropped from a bird."

"Precisely." Alfie said as it made sense to him now. "I'll go and get the General and Aggie and meet y'all back here."

A few minutes later they all appeared and the General said, "So where is this Nuclear Casing?"

Chandler pointed the direction, "Right here sir."

"Well, I'll be conky. Those retards had more up their sleeve than we thought."

Christie urged the General, "Sir, we have to investigate this base in Somalia called Sasawaha, have you ever heard of a place?"

"Nope, sure haven't but I am sure that Langely could help us out on this one. We'll need to get back to the states and figure this one out on our own. Thanks for all your help we can take this one from here. Y'all head on back to New York we'll make the arrangements for your departure and if we need you we'll call. In the meantime if you find out anything here's where you can reach me. I'll be at Langley."

He handed all of them his card and they all went back to the hotel. On the way back in the Transport Alfie and Christie were talking and Alfie offered Christie some Juicy Fruit, "You want some?"

"Thank you. Oh, look this has splenda in it."

"You know how they make splenda don't you?"

"I have never researched that one."

"Back in the days of Genghis Kahn they all had really bad breath after they would go on hunts and eat the fruits of their spoils. So Genghis called out to the God of Sugar, her name was Christie, and he prayed to her saying please oh great one would you bless us with your perfect lips and kiss the snow that you have given us so abundantly and make the spice of the God's. And Christie said for you oh Genghis I will do anything, and she kissed the snow that they were standing on and it turned into sugar or splenda. Genghis and his followers all picked up the splenda and put it on their fruits and made gum out of it and it would freshen their breath. And they lived happily ever after."

"That's a great story, and the moral is..."

"Your lips are so priceless that with a kiss you can turn snow into sugar, or splenda, and anything that comes from your lips is blessed."

"Aww, you are so sweet Alfie, I have a friend named Linda that would love that story."

"I'll have to tell it to her sometime."

"That would be great."

"And that is when they built the first Wrigley field, in Mongolia."

Langley, Virginia 4:00 pm

Kerry Carpenter was a very tall man with a round head and a chiseled face that wore the sharpest Armani Suits. His power tie today was a Safari theme with an African Landscape and tons of wildlife, with the face of a wildebeest on the very front. His office was cleaner than some of the rooms at Intel. Beside his nameplate on his desk there were pictures of his family and a card that had roses and hearts on it that said, "You had me at first sight." It must have been from his wife.

Just behind the desk was Kerry sitting in his leather chair looking out the window. He was a very gentle man who knew much in the realm of intelligence on terrorists around the world. He kept the best relationships with all of his staff and field agents who respected him a great deal. General Watson and Aggie were right down the hall walking up to his office as they saw his nameplate on the door that was wide open so they stepped in and Watson said, "Excuse me, Kerry, it's General Watson and Aggie to see you."

An Indian lady was at the front of the office who must have been his secretary said, "Don't worry about a thing, I will get him." She pressed a button on the phone and said, "Sir, you have visitors."

General Watson smiled at the lady and found her accent very amusing. He looked towards the back of the office and saw Kerry's head just above the top edge of the chair and said, "He is expecting us."

With her headset on she relayed the info, "You can go on back now." As they were walking back, out of habit she said, "Thank you, come again." Just like Aboo from the Simpson's.

They walked down the side of the room and when they arrived at his desk Kerry spun around and said warmly, "Men, great job over there in Afghanistan, I've got some field agents over there that have turned up some critical data about that base."

Kerry gestured for them to have a seat and they did in the two chairs directly in front of his desk. General Watson said with a smile, "Thanks, actually that's what we're here to talk about." He handed Kerry the reports and Kerry thumbed through them and then halted on one page in the back.

Kerry was obviously taken back by the report and its findings and said, "Great work here, it looks like there is more than one beehive out there... Sasawaha...hummm, never heard of it. Let me make a phone call real quick guys find out what we can on this."

Kerry got out a book that had letter tabs on the side then flipped through all the way to the S's. With his pen, Tiffany Mont Blanc, skimmed down till he got to the word Somalia, then over to the right side of the page. He picked up the phone and dialed, someone answered then he said, "Kawejwa can you get me everything you got on Sasawaha." He covered the phone receiver and said to the men, "This'll just be a minute."

His laptop on the desk began to flash up a ton of pictures then a satellite image came on and it zoomed to an area right outside of Mogadishu on the inland. "Yeah, it's already on the screen. Thanks a bunch Kawejwa, don't forget about our Cowboys bet you know you owe me... Alright have a good one, say hello to the wife for me. You too."

Kerry turned around the laptop so that both of them could see what was on the screen. At first he showed them the pic of some indigenous people wearing African clothing. "These are the Sasawaha tribe they are about 100 people and they are located about 40 miles west of Mogadishu."

He flipped through the screen and then settled in on paperwork that had, "CIAclopedia," on it. Kerry had never heard about these people and neither had Aggie or the General. Kerry told the men about the paper, "I did some research here and what we're looking for is shipping documents over the past few years that originated from Kudesh Hindukush Afghanistan. I have no way of accessing that but if you stay with me for a minute I can get one of my field agents that is stationed in Mogadishu to do the research for me."

"That'll work." Aggie said with hope in his voice. They had already discovered a bunch of new information and this would be, potentially, a break for them to find out where these weapons are going.

Kerry got on the phone and called over to his secretary, "Can you get me Andre Lauter?"

"Don't you worry about a ting. I'll patch him, over as soon as I reach him."

Kerry fixed his eyes on the men at his desk and said, "After we get all this do y'all want to go and get some Asian?"

The General responded without hesitation, "I am starved, that would be great. You?"

"Sure, I am pretty hungry myself. Asian sounds good to me."

Kerry adjusted his tie and General Watson noticed the wildebeest and asked, "That's quite a tie you got there, where did you get it from?"

"This was a gift from my daughter, when she went to the Congo for a field trip with her class she brought it back for me."

"That's quite a field trip."

"She is an actress and they were on this field trip on site with Stephen Speilberg's latest movie doing research."

"That's great."

"Yeah, she is my sweety."

Kerry picked up his remote and pressed a button and the TV came on and there was his daughter on the flatscreen OLED in the corner of the office. "This is a movie that they made in film school at the University. She is quite the actress, great at comedy too."

They all watched part of the movie and Aggie said, "She has such a sweet personality, she could be America's next Sweetheart."

"She's my sweety and with God she can accomplish anything."

They all sat there and talked for another hour then Kerry got the call, it was Andre. Kerry told him all the intel that they needed and Andre got to work on it and said he would call him back when he found something.

Chapter 17

Traccia's Restaurant 6:00pm

It had been quite a day for the new couple and now they were at the front of Traccia's standing in line to get to the Hostess who was a stunningly beautiful woman with a brown name tag that said, "Ella Clancy." The waiting room for Traccia's consisted of two light brown leather cushioned benches with black and white pictures of Angie's family on the brick walls. Angie was a waitress, short handed after she got back from the trip, and she came through the kitchen doors with steaming hot plates of lasagna on a tray.

After she sat down the plates she went up to the front and asked Ella, "Has Christie made it here yet?"

"Not yet."

"They are already supposed to be here. I'll go check the line."

As soon as she opened the door to the waiting room she saw them holding hands and said, "Christie y'all come on back. I gotta special table for you reserved."

Christie smiled with a full set of teeth and said, "Thanks." They proceeded to the back of the restaurant to a velvet rope section that had Tony standing guard. Just above Tony it said, "Zona Rosa." The letters were animated in a field of roses and danced across the wall.

"Tony will get you seated. I'll be right back."

Christie let go of Alfie's hand and with a huge grin said, "Hey Tony, you missed a great trip."

"I knowa, I know. You'lla have to tella me all about it." He showed them to their seats which were at a table mid way back and against the right side wall. Alfie got Christie's seat for her then sat down to a video of Tony playing on the wall next to them.

Tony was wearing a gleaming white chef's shirt with large round white cushioned buttons that tapered up on the left side of his shirt. He had on a white chef's poofy pleated hat and you could see him from the torso up with the Traccia's kitchen in the background. In his charismatic personality he talked with his distinct Italian accent, "Hey thanks for a coming to Traccia's and the new addition Zona Rosa, I'm Tony and I'll be your waiter for the night and I'll be here so if you need anything just press this tab on the screen to order. If you'll look just below me you'll see a camera that will record your order then I'll bring a it out to you. Guess what? We've got satellite so you can watch anything you like right here on the screen or feel free to upload your own videos or choose from our library of movies. Enjoy!"

Christie acknowledged Tony and said, "Thank you."

Tony was in the mood to life their spirits, "Would you like to hear some jokes before I get your order?"

"Sure Tony, that would be lovely."

"What is silent and smells like worms?"

"I don't know what?"

"Chicken farts, it must have been an engineer who designed the human body to put a waste processing plant next to a recreation area."

Alfred and Christie burst out laughing, "Do you know any more?"

"Why don't blind people go skydiving?"

"Why?"

"Scares their dogs."

"Oh goodness that's hilarious." They both rolled in laughter.

"I'll be right out after you order."

Christie was wearing a dark blue dress that had two straps that wrapped around her shoulders and formed into a beautiful bare back that came to a point just above her curvy hind quarters. She was wearing a diamond necklace that was placed just above her brilliant blooming supple breasts that formed the perfect curve when she looked to her right to see what she wanted on the menu. The menu's were on each side of the screen on the FOLED wall but Alfie already knew what he wanted as he glanced from the curvy path to the digital menu on the wall. Scan down...Lasagna, flip page...white wine, scan down...Chardonnay, scan further...Traccia's House, done.

Now to find something special for her, he had full access to the internet and a digital keyboard, he got to searching. Google search box, rose, results: a billion, scroll down with a swift of the fingertip, picture of a shoddy dressed man in an overcoat with a rose. Wait that was Columbo, one of his idols, she had to have it. Save, send as text to 434-555-7673, Chrsitie's phone, include message...one rose at a time ;-.), send, done. And... ring ring on Christie's phone as she was sifting through the menu, she looks down at her small compact matching purse, unclips, digs, finds, views the screen and wait for it, wait for it..., "Aww, Alfie you are sooo sweet. Do you know what you want?"

Alfie's eyes were on her brown beauties, then the phone, then just past it a few inches, then the response, "Oh yeah."

"Up here Alfie."

He ducked his head just a bit, then straightened up, looked her square in her brown jewels and said, "Yes dear, lasagna, House Chardonnay. And you?"

"That sounds appetizing."

"Always in the mood. Do you know what you want yet?"

"Not sure yet." Quick glance at the menu, then a tap on the screen, cheese filled lasagna, glance down at her new shoddy Columbo rose, okay she was ready, "I think I'll have the same. You know I am keeping all of these, and I will expect for you to find that silk rose that was at the Waldorf."

"Actually, I picked that silk rose up that day, before I found you in that room. Its been in my pocket ever since. Here it is." Alfie romantically said as it appeared and he gave it to her. He put a bunch of fingers on his chin, tilted his head, then finish it with a warm smile. The cutest smile back and success.

"Alfie!" She sounded like Meg Ryan in When Harry Met Sally.

"Yes, my dear."

"This is the best rose that you could ever give me, oh thank you so much."

"Know what you want now?"

"I have already found it, and yes I am getting hungry, could you order for us?"

"It'd be my pleasure, your sexiness." Alfie tapped the menu screen, order meal, pop up their faces on the main screen, then, "Tony we will have a bottle of the House Chardonnay and lasagna for the both of us. Greatly appreciated."

Pre-recorded video of Tony saying, "I'll have that out as soon as possible. Enjoy."

Christie with always something positive to say, "That was quite nice of you."

"Thank you ma'am just doing my part." In his John Wayne accent.

Before they could start talking Tony was rounding third with a bottle of wine in his hand and glasses in the other. "Great selection, it is-a my favorite choice. I've got a minute, so-a let me in on all of your adventures."

Alfie was glad to assist as Tony poured the wine, "What we've found out so far is that Al-Qaeda was planning some attack, nuclear attack on the US."

Christie elaborated, "They have nuclear missiles, but the thing is, is that we don't know where they are going to get any jets to launch them with. If an unknown jet were to fly into our airspace our Air Force would shoot them down in a mili-second."

Tony was finished pouring the glasses and he sat down the bottle on the table and said, "Well it's good to know that we are all safe. So tell me more about the romancing. Angie says that ya'll got very acquainted while you were in Afghanistan."

"Yeah, we got to know each other better of the last few days." Alfie said taking a savory sip of his wine.

Tony clapped his hands together and said, "That is wonderful, I know you guys are perfect for each other."

A waiter was at the ropes and said, "Tony we need you back here, how do you make the tortellini?"

With a terse look Tony said, "I am so sorry it seems that duty calls. Come over tomorrow, I want to hear about everything."

Christie placed her handkerchief in her lap delicately and said, "Sure, we would love to."

"I'll have the food out in just-a minute."

Alfie hadn't thought of it yet, "Who do you think would give them a jet much less a squadron?"

"Iraq and Iran both have Air Forces and I wouldn't put it past them."

"Our planes do patrol the Atlantic don't they?"

"They will now even more so."

"If they were planning anything at least we would cut them off before they could do anything."

"I wonder what they are releasing to the press?" The national anthem began to play on Christie's phone, she picked it up. "Hello."

"Christie, this is Kerry Carpenter CIA, I am sitting here with General Watson and Aggie and we just got a call and found out that there have been several shipments from Kudesh to Mogadishu and particularly Sasawaha over the last year. The indigenous people would never import anything from Afghanistan so we know that Al-Qaeda has or had some kind of base here in Somalia. All of these shipments could have been nuclear weapons, the thing is that the shipments stopped about a week ago then four days ago they exported a whole ship full of cargo to Saudi Arabia. We have no records of any activity after this."

"Thanks Kerry for letting us know, let us know if there is anything else we can do to help you out if you need it."

"Stay close, if you find out anything else you call us."

"Sure thing. Bye."

"Goodbye."

Alfie was busy listening to Christie and could hear the whole conversation and was pulling up some information about the Zona Rosa.

Christie relayed her thoughts on the conversation, "Saudi Arabia? Isn't that where Mustafa now lives."

"Yes, it is but where is he going to get a squadron of jets from?"

"I have no idea."

Alfie was indulged with the information about Zona Rosa, "It says here that the Zona Rosa comes from a book of William Gibson. Did you know that he loves his editor on a strictly ebonic level?"

"That's interesting, he's white isn't he?"

"Yes, as a cracker."

"That makes that all the more interesting."

"Oh, wait it says platonic."

"That makes more sense."

"He dedicated his last book, brilliant by the way, to his editor."

"Now that is a seasoned professional author."

"There is no one on the planet that can give such detail to their stories as Gibson."

"What is Zona Rosa though?" Christie wanted to know.

"Let me look it up on the internet...It says here that it is a part of Mexico City."

Tony was rounding the bases with steaming Lasagna on a tray. "Guys, here it isa. Fresh homemade lasagna."

"Gee, thanks Tony. Hey, what is Zona Rosa?"

"You know that William Gibson is from Vancouver and he visits here all the time for book signings so we made this part of the restaurant in honor of him. He is a great customer."

Christie said sipping some wine, "That explains the high tech stuff in here, you know this room is way cool."

"Why thanka you pretty lady. FOLED walls are the next big thing. Zona Rosa is from his book Idoru, which is a character that is a leader of a girl gang from Mexico City and from the walled city that protects the distributed system. Can I get you anything else?"

"We are fine for now. Thanks, Tony." Christie added the cutest wink in there with her comment. Tony grabbed the empty tray from the other table put it up in the air and walked off in his white garb.

Alfie got a text on his phone about one of his stocks, Universal Display, so wanting to research it he selected the Fox Business channel on the main screen on the wall. On the screen wall there was a news clip from Terraoil's stock. The news anchorman said, "Terraoil's stock has risen 19 percent since they announced their new fleet of oil tankers and plan on seeing the stock continue to rise as they tour the US for their first shipments of oil. These Tankers are nothing like the Exxon-Valdez spill or the mishap by BP earlier on this year. No, Terraoil does have several off-shore rigs around the world but they are all designed to withstand anything like we have seen from these other companies. Here is a look at one of the new Tankers on its way to Somalia. The Tankers should be making their first appearance in America in a few hours."

On the FOLED wall, main screen, Christie and Alfie watched and saw the back of the tanker as it sailed off in the Persian Gulf. On the back of the ship it said this in large yellow letters across its breadth, several feet above the water:

Terraoil
Mogadishu
Sasawaha

When they saw that Alfie went straight for his phone as did Christie. Aflie dialed General Watson's number and Christie hit previous call. They got them on the line and talked simultaneously Christie said, "Sir, they are not bombing us with jets."

"We saw the missiles Christie."

"I know, but it's not jets, its oil tankers, Mustafa's Terraoil Tankers.

That's why that shipment went to Saudi Arabia, to Terraoil. And all of those tankers are being sent to every port in the US. We have to do something."

"Okay, we only have a few hours before they dock. I'll alert the Navy and Air Force and stop any tankers from reaching their destination. This is going to be quite an orchestration but I think we can do it. Thanks for letting us know. We need you to go to the New York building so we can communicate. I'll have someone waiting on you. Bye."

"Goodbye."

Tony was there waiting on her to hangup, he typed something in his phone and a dessert menu popped up on the main screen. He noticed the look on her face and asked, "Everything okay?"

"We gotta go Tony, thanks for everything." Alfie said leaving some bills on the table and taking the last drink of Chardonnay he arose. Christie took one more bite of her Lasagna and grabbed Alfie's hand and went storming out of Traccia's. They got a Taxi and went straight to the the New York CIA building.

Chapter 18

RIYADH, SAUDI ARABIA

All eyes were on the 100 inch TV on the left wall of the meeting room at the palace of Sheik Rhyanton. Mustafa was outside the room in the hall on the phone talking to one of his chronies. There was water running at his feet down a narrow brook that lined the long grand hallway, the trickle made him nervous. Perhaps it was more than just the trickle and the sound that it made over the now smooth rocks beneath.

Mustafa kicked at the water and said, "They better be on time, we cannot afford any mishaps, no mistakes."

The voice on the other end of the phone said, "Cargo is on board and they will be in for a great show. There is no way of the US finding out about this, it doesn't matter if one of them is late. This will be a global catastrophe compared to 911. 911 was just the beginning this is the end."

"Of Western civilization period."

"They rebuilt from 911 they will have nothing to rebuild with after this one."

"You better hope so."

"I know so."

"Very good then, I will call you when we have arrivals. It will be all over the news."

They hung up the phone and Mustafa went into the meeting room where the Sheik was gathered around the table with some of his partners. Rhyanton shifting his smile towards Mustafa said, "This will go off without a bang."

Mustafa started chuckling and said, "I don't know about that."

"Our stock will only go higher after their arrival is broadcast all over the world and they see the fleet that I have amassed."

The Sheik, primary owner and CEO of Terraoil, knew nothing of what Mustafa had done and was merely hoping that this showing of his new fleet would raise his stock. He would be in for a rude awakening when he finally saw on TV what was about to happen. The Sheik was a short man with a beard nicely groomed and a green turban and the one thing that attracted his harem to him was his wallet and the shopping sprees they would all go on in the states.

Rhyanton took a drink of his water, no ice, and said, "I love America, if it weren't for their consumers the entire oil industry would be out of business."

Mustafa had some pertinent history as he adjusted his shoddy suit and said, "After World War II the American consumers started buying cars like crazy and then by the end of the decade the entire oil industry went kaboom."

Terraoil had on board cameras installed that documented their journey to the states and all of the men were watching the deck and the waters ahead. Every ship was set to arrive in about an hour, so they were getting close, and Rhyanton wanted to observe every part of the operations. The tanker that was headed to the Houston port had already crossed under the Florida peninsula and it was the closest one to American soil.

The Sheik combed his beard, "Someone call the Houston ship and ask if the fireworks are ready."

Mustafa grinned then grimmaced and said to the men with his arms raised, "This will be the largest fireworks show in history."

One of the partners said, "I cannot wait."

Mustafa put his hand on his chin and said, "Neither can I."

Chapter 19

LANGLEY VIRGINIA 6:28PM

Kerry's office was a buzz sparked by a litter of calls that brought people in and out of his office non stop since he got the call from Christie. Kerry knew what had to be done and as the video of the tanker played in his office TV he asked General Watson, "Can you get enough birds up there to head them off?"

General Watson knew rank and command better than anyone and tapped out a cadence on the mahogany chair rails and said nervously, "We have to get authorization from the top on this one before we can proceed to use a large fraction of our guys up in the air."

"Can you make that call?"

"We're also going to need the Navy in on this one. Yes, I'll make the call."

"Good I'll be getting sat imagery on all of the vessels locations and headings."

General Watson got out his cell phone and scrolled his address book and found Barak Obama, Oval Office. He tapped it. The President answered and said, "This is Barak."

"Mr. President this is General Watson Air Force and we have intel at the CIA that over 34 known nuclear weapons on board Terraoil tankers that are currently in transit to 34 coastal cities in the US. This is a full scale attack by Al-Qaeda and we must stop them by sea and by air. Do I have your permission to use fighter jets and helicopters to stop this attack?"

"How do we know that there are nuclear weapons aboard?"

"It's a long story but I can assure you they are equipped with nuclear weapons, I'll send you the full report right now."

"If you can prove to me that there is one oil tanker that has a nuclear weapon on it then I'll grant you the use of those jets. Not a moment sooner. How much time till they reach the coast?"

"One hour and 28 minutes and they are all on schedule."

"That should give you enough time if this is what we think it is. I'll give the Navy the same orders. Very good."

"Goodbye."

Aggie who was sitting next to him asked as Kerry buzzed on the phone, "Did we get the go ahead?"

"The Houston bound tanker first. I gotta talk to Norton." The General scrolled through his phone found him and tapped.

"Norton Schwartz here."

"Norton, this is Watson, we need to send a squadron of attacks and helicopters, and the best paratrooper to the Gulf."

"There a problem?"

"Uhh, yeah nukes on Terraoil tankers, 34 of them."

"You get the go?"

"Yeah."

"I'll send them. Goodbye."

"Bye."

Chapter 20

Moody AFB Georgia

Air Force Major Lee Erdon had just called in his team and they were assembled, sitting and standing around in a new meeting facility on the Moody Air Force Base. Sitting front and center was Senior Airman George Putnam. He was known to be the best in the business when it came to accurate landings in the Paratrooper division and won every game on the base.

Glad to get this opportunity to serve Major Lee summoned the troops, "We have intel that there is a fleet of oil tankers that are an hour and 20 minutes from bombing every port in the US. Men I don't know about you, but I'm not gonna let that happen. We are going to board their tankers and disarm their nukes and we're gonna need your help to make this happen. Paratroopers you've been training for this, Putnam, Fortis, Jacob, and Day you've been selected to make this happen. You leave now. It's an honor to serve. Hooah!"

The troops resounded with a reverberating, "Hooah!"

The Chinese fire drill resulted in a quick trot to their planes, a stomp up the ramp and sooner than you knew it they were airborne. Their CO was in the back of the plane with them and prepping them for their mission. Putnam was busy packing his parachute when the CO First Lieutenant Edward Smokoob started briefing him on their procedure. "Pack it good this is all riding on you."

"I'll do my best. You know that."

"It's a tandem jump."

"Tandem what the heck?"

"You will be strapped to bomb expert John Blussh."

"Tandem?"

"What did you think, you were just going to dismantle it yourself?"

"I didn't know alright."

"Can you do it?"

"It's an honor to serve, and you know I could land on a dime."

"That's why I chose you Putnam. Day will be taking along someone else too."

"Well, that's just great let's take along the President while we're at it."

"You think you could do it?"

"I took the training, cut the right wire snip snip, and boom no babies."

"Well this guy has done this thing his entire career."

"Professional vaginologist that's great. I don't think it's that tough though."

"No, what if there's a catch wire designed for you to clip it and it sets off a timer and you've got no lift outta there?"

"I heard it's Iranian, you actually think those guys are that smart?"

"Will you do it? Simple yes or no."

He shrugged with no answer and continued packing.

"If you won't I've got ten other guys who are ready and waiting. They would be more than happy to get a chance at this."

"Alright."

"Is that a yes?"

Putnam punched the soft cushion of the chute. "Yes, I'll do it."

"Good be ready and strapped in ten. You jump in 18. I'll introduce you."

The Airman Blussh had been listening so walked up and said, "I'm about as thrilled about this monkey jump as you."

"Well that makes two of us."

Lt. Edward finished up, "And they lived happily ever after." He walked over to Airman Day to tell him of the great news and almost tripped over Putnam's outstretched knee that was there for a sendoff. The Lt. Just looked back and said nothing. Putnam knew he had gotten to him.

"Day guess what? It's your lucky day."

"I think it is, sir."

"I've got you jumping with Leeland Jarrett a weapons expert. He is Blussh's back up, we shouldn't need him. That okay with you?"

"No problems here. Glad to do it, sir."

"Good you jump in 15 be ready."

"Will do, sir." He stood at full attention and saluted.

"Keep your chin up, I like your attitude, I just wish everyone around here had the same outlook."

"I do my best, sir."

"Very good, carry on." The Lt. Saluted back and Day got to work.

After awhile they were all strapped up and ready to go. The back hydraulics were down and they were standing on the line there was a red light on, covered by a few strips of iron, they were waiting on the green. They were lined up with Putnam and Blussh first then Day and Jarrett and the other two behind them. The two bomb experts traded redundancies just before jumping yelling through the wind. The sun was setting and it would be pitch dark on the vessel by the time they landed.

The light went green and the Lt. Sent them off with a, "Go, go, go, go!"

In a second Putnam's chute opened and looking down he could see the speck of a few lights that were the Terraoil tanker. The speck grew larger and he adjusted is chute for the wind variance. The speck now was much larger and Putnam could see the helipad so he made more adjustments shifting his hands down and up. They were ready to land and were in good accurate position as he shifted his weight towards the big H in the circle. This was going to be a successful landing he thought as he approached noticing no wind variance.

Ten yards before touchdown a gale wind violently gusted them to the side making them way off target. Putnam cursed and adjusted vigorously with all his might to realign themselves then just when it looked like they were going to land in the Gulf another gust of wind blew them to the far side of the ship. Their feet hit the deck stinging, then another gust whisked them overboard. They would surely fall into the Gulf of Mexico. Their blue and yellow chute's cords went plummeting over the railing, the two men went dashing towards the water.

The cords looked like they might get tangled in the railing hook but they just kept falling. Part of the trailing chute went past the hook and it seemed that they were goners. Then the most unlikely thing happened a gale force wind blew the chute on the deck right into the hook and the jolt went rippling through the cords and Putnam and Blussh were violently jerked back and were dangling there just above the top of the ocean.

The other tandem landed right on the H and had seen what was happening so they detached and ran over to the chute that was flapping in the wind. The other two singles landed, detached quickly and ran over to their aid. Another gust of wind whipped the chute around and Jarrett and Day did what they could to grab it before they went into the sea.

Day called out, "Danm it, grab the chute!"

Fortis grabbed a hold and just as Jacob got a grip it whisked out of his hands. He ran over to the part of the deck where Fortis and Day were standing and grabbed hold, they weren't about to let them be shark bait. Day yelled out to Putnam, "We've got you, don't do anything."

The tanker was coming up close on an offshore drilling rig and Putnam saw this and before Day could say anything else Putnam detached and fell into the water. Day looked back at the guys and said to Jarrett, "You can do this, we just have to find it first."

Fortis' blood was pumping, "Yeah, before we hit that rig."

The rig was getting closer and closer and they didn't have much time so they all scattered about the ship and pulled out their equipment. Jarrett said to himself, "Where could it be?"

Day yelled out to the guys that were now yelling at the Arabs that were running the ship, "It is here, tell them who we are, ask them if they know where it is."

Fortis just nodded as Day went running towards the reserve tank below deck. Day had a hunch that these ships were empty and a few steps down the ladder he saw the tops of the tank battery. He got out his gun knowing that a bullet would just bounce off and fired it hoping to hear what was inside. "Ting."

"Aha. They are empty."

There were about ten of them all lined up next to each other with hatches on the tops of them. He went to the first hatch and pulled out his flashlight. "Nothing." It was empty nothing in the base of it so he went to the next one. Meanwhile Fortis was still attempting to talk to the Arabs knowing no Arabic at all he drew a picture of a bomb with a notebook from his pack.

Sweating profusely Fortis' eyebrow was like the rocks on the top of a waterfall, needless to say his adrenaline was pumping at all of the commotion. Pointlessly he said to the towel heads, "There is a bomb somewhere on this ship. Do you know anything?" He pointed correlating with his words. They were getting closer to the oil rig that was dead ahead of the front of the ship.

Fortis got frustrated and threw the notebook and pen down and went down the ladder and yelled out to day. "We've got about six minutes till impact and we all could be toast."

"I'm still looking."

"Found anything?"

Sarcastically Day said, "Seriously." Then he went to the next battery flashlight in hand.

Fortis looked up and there were the Arabs standing on deck with the notebook. They were motioning to him and saying something he couldn't understand, but they did have smiles on their faces. There was another guy one of the deck hands that was with them this time and he must have known something because when Fortis got up the ladder the guy was jumping in the air. He was pointing at the bomb on the notebook saying something in a high pitched voice, looked like an idiot with a gargantuan grin, when his mouth was closed.

Fortis looked pleased and asked, "Where is it?" They said something and then proceeded to walk away towards the back stowaway section of the ship. When Fortis saw where they were going He leaned down the ladder and said to day, "We found it."

"Be right there. Get Jarrett!"

"Okay."

With Blussh and Putnam swimming towards the rig that kept on getting closer Fortis located Jarrett and motioned for him to join the Arabs. He came running over to him and asked, "You found it?"

"I don't know, I'm just following these guys."

"Goodness any minute now and we are going to run right into that rig."

"I know, I know. Lets just pray that they know where it is."

Day followed up the rear and said, "Well where is it?"

"Stowaway."

"Stowaway?"

"One of the containers." As the jumping Arab pointed to the top container.

"Let's do this. Jarrett you first." Jarrett hesitated for a minute. "You afraid of heights?"

He didn't say anything, Day pointed to the rig that was right up on them. "Toast or toast?" Day motioned with his hands like an explosion then motioned like he was clanging glasses and drinking something.

"Okay, I'll do it." Jarrett began to climb.

He got a few steps up and Day said to him, "You're gonna need this."

He handed him a crowbar and Jarrett secured it in his pack both ends hanging out. "Thanks."

When he got up to the top he found a cubed wooden crate and asked, "What am I looking for." Standing on the top trying to stay centered.

"Sasawaha."

"Right...this is it." He dug his crowbar with a whack and cut into the wood. After he had eaten his way through the wood and packing he got out something that looked like a saw and some sparks went up in the air. "Found it. Got to get to the wires first."

Shaking his head with a huge smile Day said, "Do what you do and lets get outta here." Day noticed how close the rig was getting and asked, "Jacob you get up there in the control room and steer us away from that rig. I'm gonna notify Major Lee and let him know we found it."

Jacob dusted off the foam from the packing that had blown on his suit and said, "Yes, sir." Day called in to Lee and let him know, which sent off a chain reaction throughout the intelligence community and down the ranks of the Navy and Air Force. Jacob took off running and climbed up the steps and found that the room was bolted shut. Jacob was acclimated to improvisation and got out his gun and did some impromptu of his own. The door swung open and he pointed the 9mm directly at the head of the Captain, then motioned him to move. Just behind him was another worker that lunged his gun into the back of Jacob's neck. Apparently there were two teams of people working on this rig, those who knew something and those who knew nothing and were friendly. These weren't the friendly kind.

As all of the guys were watching Jarrett go to work Jacob yelled out, "Somebody better get over here!"

Day reloaded and fired a shot from a distance in the direction of the guy that had Jacob hostage. Running over, Day and Fortis fired off some more shots then the door closed again, sparks went shooting in every which direction around the door. Day nodded over to Fortis and the hatched a plan together. When Day got there he kicked in the door and put his 9mm right in the ear of the Arab. The other Arab pointed his gun at Day and just when it looked like the Americans were outmatched, Fortis kicked in the door on the other side and fired off a shot into the ceiling to let them know he was there then buried the end of the gun in the other Arab's head.

Day was relieved and said with confidence, "We got you bastards now."

Immediately they dropped their weapons, Day and Fortis marched them over to the containers while Jacob started pulling on the steering wheel. Dead and center was the rig and as he pulled they slowly went from going directly at the center to the right leg of the rig. They were moving too fast though, Jacob had done all he could do.

Meanwhile the guys were back over at the bomb and Day asked Jarrett, "Almost got it?"

"I found the right wire."

"Well clip it and lets go the choppers just landed."

"It's complicated I have never seen anything like this I'm not sure what this will do."

"You're supposed to be the expert, you want me to get up there."

"I don't know."

In disgust Day said, "Goodness gracious, you're gonna make me climb all the way up there." Day started his ascent and was up there in no time. Just has he positioned himself in a safe working corner Jarrett clipped the wire that he had been contemplating about.

"You got it?" Day had this complex relieved and puzzled look on his face.

"Yeah. That's it." Jarrett said with a smile.

Then as the two men were climbing down they heard this beep. Day said, "Oh great." Then they climbed back up and noticed that there were now number flashing on the screen. "This thing is gonna blow, yall get to the choppers."

They didn't move. Day said again, "Get to the choppers or I'll shoot you right here. That's an order."

Reluctantly Fortis and Jacob went off for the choppers Day stayed around to talk to Jarrett. "Now do you know what to do?"

"I'm pretty sure that if I clip this one it will disarm the damn thing."

"Well do it." The ship's steering wheel was turned as far to the right as it would go, Jacob rigged it that way with a prayer. Apparently God answers prayers because when the nose of the tanker got to the right leg it averted disaster and the left side went skidding along the overhanging rig floor. It missed a dead on collision, but the impact of the skid was sending the ship to lean to one side as Jarrett steadied his grip on the clippers and Day hung on to the crate for dear life.

Day was slipping and yelled out to Jarrett, "Cut the damn thing already."

"Okay, okay." He made the snip and...

"Did you?"

"Yeah."

"So what happened?"

"The screen went blank."

"Way to go there buddy, now lets get the heck outta here."

They climbed down and the guys were waiting in the chopper which was starting to lean pretty steep with the side of the ship being railed by the rig. The contact point was getting close to the center of the tanker where it bows out the most and was climbing to the top railing steadily. This sent the ship on even more of a tilt and the helicopters had to take off leaving Jarrett and Day running up a steep embankment as the ship was capsizing. The Coast Guard chopper let down two ropes that were blowing to one side in the fierce winds. Just before the tilt got to be too much the two men grabbed onto the side railing of the ship and stood on the top of it balancing themselves in the wind.

The pilot of the chopper noticed the lean of the ropes in the wind and adjusted his course directly above the two balancing acts. Just when the rope came within grasp of Day he jumped and grabbed hold of it and the team started to spin his rope up. Now it was Jarrettes turn, The chopper adjusted it's course again and the rope went flying by Jarrett, he reached, then slipped his footing. He said a quick prayer and the rope miraculously swung back to him just before he fell into the Gulf. They pulled him up and all but Putnam and Blussh were safe.

The chopper immediately rose above the tilt of the side of the ship and flew around to where they had seen the two men last. When the pilot got there, there was nothing, no Airmen floating around so they decided to circle the rather large offshore rig again. Just as they got around to the back side Day, out of the side window, noticed Putnam jumping around and waving his arms on the rig floor. Blussh was still climbing the ridiculously long ladder.

Day said in his comm system, "There they are."

The pilot answered back, "Where? I don't see them anywhere."

"On the rig floor main level."

"Okay, they're safe. We'll let Major Lee know where they are and he can schedule a pickup for them. Let's get the heck outta here. Whatdaya say?"

Day was just glad to be in the air again, "Let's go."

Chapter 21

NEW YORK CIA OFFICE

It was a glittering night littered by the speckled lights around the area of town that they were in. The streets weren't crowdly buzzing nor were there faint stragglers. There were signs of nightlife going to their destinations outside the taxi as they pulled up to the building. The gentleman that he was, Alfie got out some more bills, and generously handed it to the driver, as he smiled through an overgrown mustache and said, "Thanks, you be careful out there."

Getting out Alfie ducked his head back in the cab and said, "We will, thanks for the ride."

He took Christie's hand and she stepped out and closed her arms close together due to the chill. There were a group of people walking by and one of the women looked at Alfie who almost bumped into her and he heard, "Excuse me."

Alfie took off his coat and placed it around Christie's shoulders and ignored the rude woman. "This is the place." They looked around towards the entrance then scanned up to the top floor of the building and Alfie put his hand at her back waist and they proceeded towards the front door. The building name and insignia were clad in stainless steel on glass to their right they walked past towards the guard dressed in black.

It appeared that there were always the usual guards or CIA bouncers around the entrance. Alfie thought, "Sunglasses at night? Can you say overkill? I guess it's standard protocol."

As they got to the door the CIA bouncer stepped in front of them with a wand and said, "Step this way. I'll need to see some ID."

"Sure, of course."

As they were getting scanned by the wand they both got out their ID's, New York state driver's licenses. Alfie was first and it beeped on him so he took out his keys then he was fine. It didn't beep on Christie and as they were putting their ID's back in their place the guard asked, "Is someone expecting you?"

Alfie put his wallet up in his coat pocket on Christie and said, "Kerry Carpenter from Langley said someone would be expecting us."

"Just walk on through to the front desk and someone will be right with you."

It was much warmer in the lobby area and the lady at the front desk was very friendly not cold like many government places. She said, "Who are you here for?"

Christie spoke up and said, "Kerry Carpenter and General Watson from Langley said that there would be someone waiting on us once we got here."

"That will be Sarah Awelay she is head of our anti terrorist division here in New York. I just spoke with her and she said that she will be right down so you can wait over there if you want. We have public wifi but don't go hacking into our systems or databases please."

"Thanks, we'll just wait over here."

They heard a ding and it was the elevator then from around the corner the most beautiful CIA woman that Alfie had ever seen walked towards them. "Sarah Awelay, you must be Alfred and Christie, nice to meet you. Come with me."

Alfie was troubled between letting Christie see his jaw drop and holding in his urge to hit on her. Christie got one look at where his eyes were when Sarah was walking in front of them and she squeezed his hand. The urge went away immediately. Sarah was very quick in her talking and didn't give them much of a chance to say anything, as if they really needed to at this point anyway.

She kept talking, "So I heard about your discovery, you know you were right. They found a nuclear bomb on the Houston tanker, it was disarmed and all of the men made it out just fine. The President heard about it and immediately gave the go ahead to launch an all out recon attack on all of the tankers in their fleet."

They were now on her floor and walking towards her office. I guess it was all of the emotions from the news, but Christie got the hiccups and went to the water fountain to control them. Whaddya know the water was so cold she couldn't possibly drink enough to get the hiccups to stop.

"We are now 40 minutes out from reaching the tankers, our Navy was deployed into action and a team..."

"Hiccup." Christie let out another one.

"Our Air Force specialists were also sent out to reach them before they get to the ports."

"Hiccup." There it was again. They were now in the office area of many TV's on the walls with cubicles scattered around. All of the offices that were on the sides of the main office area were frosted except for Sarah's. Once they went in Alife and Sarah sat down and Christie asked, "Can I have some bottled water or a coke or something? I have the Hiccups."

"Some say water some say sugar." Sarah got up and opened the fridge behind her and pulled out a coke. "How about a coke, I'll get some sugar too just in case." There were packets of splenda next to her coffee maker in a cup. She got a handful of them out and handed all of it to her.

"Hiccup. Thank you so much." Christie chugged the coke then opened the splenda and poured it on her tongue then washed it down with the coke and repeated several times. "Hiccup."

"I'll get Kerry on the phone, I know he wants to talk to you both."

She scrolled on her smart phone and pressed and started talking, "Kerry I have Christie and Alfred here with me."

"Let me talk to Christie."

"Okay, here she is." Sarah handed the phone over to Christie.

"Christie?"

"Yes, this is Christie."

"I cannot thank you enough, you know you were right about everything. If you hadn't seen what you did on that tanker, well I just can't thank you enough. You saved us all and I hope you know that."

"I am glad I could help." Sarah put it on speakerphone.

"And you most certainly have. All of those tankers are close enough to our port cities that if...if something were to go wrong right now they would all still be within the radius of the blast zone and cause considerable destruction to every city."

"We had two hours from the time that I called."

"I know, but the President wanted to send only one team out to make sure that there was a bomb on board before he launched an all out blitz on those tankers for diplomatic reasons."

"They will get to them before they detonate right?" Alfie asked with a concerned look on his face.

"Right now that is what we are hoping but we don't know. Anything could happen between now and the time that we reach them. One wrong clip and it could detonate, or whoever is behind all this could press the button and they all could explode."

"Let's just hope that doesn't happen."

"Is there anything that we can do now?"

"You have already done your part, the most we can do now is pray."

"Alright we will start praying."

"As we speak there is a team of Army Rangers set out on a course to intercept Mustafa Hasbaland in Rhiyad. Pray that they get to him before he does anything to set off those bombs."

"We will."

"I have to get back to work, but Sarah will show you some real-time videos of our troops in action. Thank you all again. Goodbye."

There were several TV's in Sarah's office including her laptop which she turned so Alfie could see. "Here are the Army Rangers approaching Rhiyad. They should be arriving at the Terraoil headquarters momentarily. I'll put this up on the other screens so all of us can see their progress."

Chapter 22

Army Rangers Intercept Mustafa

Rhiyad Saudi Arabia

There were four hummers, standard coyote brown issue, making their way towards the Terraoil Headquarters in west Rhiyad. Each Hummer carried six Rangers and there was a growing concern among the majority that they weren't going to get to Mustafa before he activated the detonation switch. Most of them had heard of how insane this Mustafa was and knew that he could do anything. Their main concern was that there were lives at stake back home and some of those lives included close family members and friends. The last thing that they wanted was for that evil bastard to do anything foolish.

One of the Rangers that was in the back of one of the Hummer's was First Lt. Charles Jones who was an IT Guru and communications specialist. He was under the notion that if they could disable Mustafa's communications that he could render the detonation device useless. Achieving this would be a feat altogether monumental to say the least. None the less he was given the orders to, while on the road, and in combat, disable all communications to the Headquarters.

You could always shut down the power, but if the device wasn't connected to the lan power grid then that wouldn't work. The key was to know the device and that was something that he didn't know. However, what he did know from all of his training in the various Army schools was that most devices that were used for detonation would transmit the signal, if from another continent, through the internet.

This facet was paramount to his game plan, you see what he thought was that if he could find the I.P. Address of this device then he could just use the US gov. backbone and shut the sucker down. That is, of course, if this device used the internet. If it didn't then it would mean that they would have to resort to gorilla warfare and just take the freaking thing from the bastard.

That was something that he was hoping that he could help them avoid, so he hacked away using all of the resources of the CIA from his laptop computer, it ran on roaming the Rhiyad wireless network. His hunch was that he could find something like this device on the Terraoil network. This such network included everything from rig monitoring to employee email. While rig monitoring wasn't any main concern he decided to check Mustafa's email and once he found the Terraoil Mustafa node then he could find all links to that node, and then, perhaps the detonator.

That was the plan anyway, but finding this would not be just a matter of finding one node then going to all the branches. No, this would require much more than that, and this was what he was in the process of doing when they arrived at the road to Terraoil. Up ahead in the distance at the length of the headlights were guard posts the side of the caleche road. As the caravan drove past, Hummer one noticed a sleeping guard in a chair, by the time that Hummer four passed the post the guard was on the phone. No worries right, they are almost there to save the day. Think again, you see this guard was calling the next post station, who called the main security.

Great, now we have an all out alert on watch for four Hummers coming their way. Would they be ready would our men be ready? After about the third round of ammo to be vanished in the post stations on the way, yeah you could say that they were both ready. Ready to die? Well let's leave that one up to their Sunday school teachers. Nonetheless they pumped ammo outta those AK's and M-16's like it was water, only these kind of stung when they hit you and they could leave you laying in a puddle of your own blood. Kind of different? Slightly, this didn't stop them from squeezing the trigger though.

The Rangers weren't really concerned with killing or not killing those freaking guards, no, their main one was on getting that detonator. If it meant killing a few towel heads in the process, so be it. Now they had made it past several posts along the way and they were approaching the main gated entrance. This was where the big guns on top of the Hummer's came into play. The gunner man in Hummer one readied himself, gripping the handles, and taking aim at the tall tower posts. From about 100 yards out he annihilated all of the freaking bozo's that were up there with AK's thinking they could take out four Hummer's.

Next was the cou de' tah, the Ranger gunner would blast his way right through the front gates disabling the motor that ran the thing, then he would duck down and let the front of the Hummer do the rest. And that's about how it happened only the gate got stuck in the main top gun and they ended up dragging the thing right through to the fountain. The far edge of the attached gate rammed the head of the Sheik's statue of himself, aww what a pity.

Hummer one just heard some loud noises, but Hummer four saw the whole thing and for those Rangers, well they just thought that was one of the funniest things they had ever seen. Now it was those same endorphin amped Rangers that would use their top gun for other purposes. They had to get through the front door so they just shot their welcome right in. Once the door was breached most of them got out of the Hummers accept for the gunners and First Lt. Charles Jones. He stayed back hacking away still doing what he could to disarm that freaking thing, not so they wouldn't have to spare some innocent civilian Terraoil employees. No, so that they wouldn't waste anymore ammo, well nobody actually asked him that, but he could be that calloused.

While Charles hacked away, most of the other Rangers were securing the compound in search, silent movie music, for the great Mustafa. Pretty much it was find him, kill him if you have to, and destroy the damned detonator. Lady on the railroad track music, or Ride of the Valkyrie, or even maybe if you're up for it enough, The Theme to the Lone Ranger. No that would be too...what's the word? Freaking geekily superfluous, okay now that's the phrase. Too much Ranger in any scene is just freaking geekily superfluous and we're going for funny here so it would have to be the Lady in distress music, have you ever heard those silent movies music? Well if you have that would be funny music for a bunch of Rangers putting bullets in towel heads.

Not that I have anything against the towel heads, but they are the bad ones in this book so they just have to die. Okay back to the action inside the compound. The Rangers were just walking through the hallway with the running water when a man in a turban popped out of the meeting room door. He had something in his hand so they all pounced on him with a new bullet clad vest, I mean chest. Unfortunately for him, the Rangers only noticed that it was only a cell phone that he had, and the worst threat he could have been would be to throw it at them.

Nonetheless, blood was in the water stream in the hall, note to perch in the water, so no animals are harmed in the making of this book, "Don't breathe in the blood of the man in the turban...unhealthy."

Now the thing is, is that there are several of the board members in that room. The Rangers, at this point don't know if one of them is Mustafa or not, so they have no clue if the men from the voices that they hear through the door have guns or not. They would soon find out, muzzle first. Luckily for the, wealthy beyond imagination, men with turbans on their heads, the muzzle first infantry Ranger didn't shoot first and ask questions later. No, what he did was, get out a mirror, standard issue for urban warfare, and tape it to the muzzle to see behind the door. And what did he see? Several turbans, of various colors, just above the top of the table.

The MacGyver of the Ranger group that taped the mirror to his muzzle was Corporal Gus Rogers, and Gus, after seeing this said to the rest of them standing around, "No guns."

The Ranger just behind him that wasn't so sure of that, only because he didn't have a mirror on his muzzle, was Sargent Kellen Heller. Well at least that's what all of the others called him, and he then said, "How do you know?"

Then, with the poor Arabs about to lose control of their bladder, from all of the fear, Gus gives the gun to Kellen. Kellen sees the same freaking thing, so he motions for the rest of the Rangers that are about to enter the room to cease fire, all with proper military gestures of course. It was pretty much him taking out a bullet holding it up in the air and then pointing his index finger in the air and moving it side to side, real proper military stuff. Anyway Gus goes in and starts screaming at the tabletop turban chickens, "Do not shoot and we will not shoot you. Do you understand?"

Their beady little Arab eyes popped out above the table and one of the poor Arabs did actually lose control of his bladder after he heard Gus. Pretty much none of them move so Gus says, "Put your hands in the air where we can see them, we will not shoot." Immediately all of their curry soaked hands shot up in the air.

The Rangers are all still standing outside watching blood stream down the water in the hall. Gus, after saying all this, takes the MacGyver mirror off his muzzle and walks in the room, and moves his gun from side to side in the direction of all of the eight men that were standing there with their orange stained palms in the air. The Arab that lost control of his bladder was wearing this dress thing, pretty much an Arab toga, that was now nicely decorated with yellow embellishments on it.

Gus knows what Mustafa looks like from all of the briefings that they drilled into his thick skull, and as he looks beneath the turbans of these Amigos he doesn't find the great moron Mustafa. So monkey see, monkey say, Gus relayed the info back to the Rangers standing in the hall of Arab blood streams, "He's not here."

Kellen was not the leader of the group by any means, but he was the next one in line to the door so he in all his infinite wisdom says, "Well, ask the bastards where the heck he is." Simple right? One of those, "Oh yeah, I should have thought of that's."

Inside the Holy Ghost revival look alike meeting room, the Arabs with their hands in the air see MacGyver Gus put down his AK on the table, so he could start on some negotiating. So Pete and Repeat walk in a bar and Repeat says to the spirit filled Holy rollers, "Where is Mustafa?"

The Katherine Kuhlman converts just stood there with their cumbaya hands in the air and didn't say as much as a dumb church mouse. Gus gets this, Indiana Jones, "I have ways of making you talk," grin on his face and picks his rifle back up and the FBI and Florida Gators light bulb dings above his head, "I will start shooting you bastards one by one if you don't tell me where Mustafa is, got it?" Nothing, "Got it? Speak up, I know you know English."

In the most serious cultured Arab accent the Sheik finally decides to save his own life and says, "We do not know."

Gus, who had been on other missions before, but never seen or done anything downright brutal before, gets this pah-sycho John Wayne Casey instinct and said, "That's not good enough!" Then, the inner John Wayne Casey in him aimed his AK at the yellow spot on the boardman's dress and fired. It hit him in the leg, missing his femoral artery, couldn't tell though because for all indications the femoral was a fem-mural of yellow and red. What a nice start for a mural dress, Gus thought, not really but it's just about as sadistic as the John Wayne Casey instinct that prompted him to shoot the bladder problemed Arab in the first place.

Now this shooting really sent fear into the hearts of the towel heads and once again more bladder problems resulted in yellow spots in these board members dresses. As these quivering dark skinned billionaires embellished their wardrobe there was a ringing of the phone. The Sheik picks it up off the table and answers it. This was perturbing to Gus so he said to the bunch, "Okay, buddy I am on a strict time schedule here and we don't have time for business calls, make it quick."

"Okay, I am talking to Mustafa." The Sheik covers the phone and says to Gus, "I will find out where he is."

"Now we're getting somewhere. Good work Sheik."

Peanuts parents filled the air in Gus's mind as he listened to the Sheik talk. Wah wah, he understood nothing, not because he wasn't paying attention like Charlie Brown, no, it was the other language thing that got him. Gus just thought, "This bozo better be close, we don't have much time, is that brownies? Something smells good. What's that noise? Oh its my stomach, damn I'm hungry. Hurry the heck up and hang up Trojan man Ryan. I can't believe I shot an AK right into that Arab's leg, that must have hurt. I am thinking too much, hurry up..."

The Sheik was off the phone, finally, but what did he say Charlie Brown Gus, over here, had no clue, Inspector Gadget would know. The Sheik looked over to Gus who was eying the stack of brownies on the back table. "I found out where he is."

"Well, spill it money bags."

"He is close, if you go out the back door there is a communication tower in the Northwest corner of the compound."

Gus was already over at the snacks table getting some to go then with a sugary Hooters mouthful he said, "Thanks. Sorry about your dresses." His mouth looked like he was missing a few teeth clad with gooey brownies. Then they were all gone, one of the soldiers that took their 6 almost tripped over the dead Arab perch food man. Through the back door and out in the backyard they spotted the comm tower. They secured the perimeter like the Rangers they were, then Gus and Kellen went in the main door while the others waited at the exit, just in case.

In the first room it looked like an office with a few computers scattered around like seeds on fertile ground. No one, not a soul, he must be in the tower. Gus yelled out to the Rangers outside, "Secure!" Then four of them ran in and secured the area. Gus went towards the stairs putting his gloved hand on the railing. A shot rang out and sparked right next to his glove pinging off the metal railing.

Gus looked up the staircase and saw a flash of a rifle darting back. Gus fired at it, whoever this was, was gone, disappeared into the upper room. AK first, head up, Gus trounced up the stairs clanging with every step a soft ting, from a rock that must have gotten stuck in his rubber sole on the way to the tower. Kellen trailed keeping a sharp eye on the upper room looking at his grip only in quick flashes.

Halfway up the stairs at the clearing Gus had gotten pretty paranoid that a bullet was about to pierce his standard issue helmet and leave his brains draining out on the stairs beneath. He yelled, "Mustafa you cannot escape we have the entire tower surrounded. You're either going to hand us the detonator of not leave here alive. What's it gonna be?"

Mustafa was not shaken, "You don't scare me with your Brittney Spears fake boobs American pride."

They continued up the stairs and when they made it to the last few steps Gus placed his AK on the ledge that was the floor of the upper room. There was Mustafa, sitting in his chair with his back to the Rangers. His head perched just above the top, his feet dangling just above the floor around the sprawl spokes of the chair. What he was doing was uncertain. Gus got ansy, "We have you surrounded, put down your gun."

Now both Gus and Kellen were standing, guns straight at Mustafa's head, on the upper room floor. Mustafa spins around with an AK in his hands, trigger finger gripped. Gus calmly said, "We have you surrounded bitch."

Gus got out his mirror and shoved it on the floor, hitting the chair of Mustafa, "You don't believe me? Look at your head Mustafa. Those aren't radioactive freckles." Mustafa looked at his face and there were about 10 red dots of light on his face. Most through the window and a few through the window in the back door.

"Take your shot then."

"No, slide me the detonator."

"I can't do that. You see this is freedom for my people. I hold a revolution in my hands, and for you well you just have guns. You can kill only one man, whereas I can kill millions."

"I have a family and friends back in one of those cities you bastard."

"Maybe your president shouldn't have done what he did. If your presidents weren't so concerned with thinking with their other head they might have mercy on my people. Instead it's Cigars and interns like Monica that get their attention. What do we have to do to get your president's attention? Huh? Tell me. If it takes killing millions of innocent pathetic lives then so be it."

"You can't let this happen."

Mustafa flipped up the plastic case over the detonator switch a red spring button closed in on his thumb. "All it takes, the answer to all of my prayers, Allah will reward me in Heaven, and most of all, my people will be free."

"There are other ways of getting freedom. Heck move to America don't bomb it."

"Feeble minds, that is not the freedom that I want, to be ruled by sadistic people, that is not freedom. You are the threat to my people. We will be united at last."

"Don't do it, we will make you a compromise, your freedom in exchange for the detonator."

"You actually think that they are just going to let me go free? Even if I die this will free them so I must."

Mustafa turned around in his chair where Gus and Kellen couldn't see him. They rushed over to him and when Gus Rogers got over there he saw over Mustafa's shoulder, his thumb press down on the button. It was over they are all dead now.

"Let me show you something, here is satellite view of the United States, notice the large mushroom clouds over the port cities. It has begun."

Gus saw the destruction on the screen just as he had said 33 mushroom clouds rising into the atmosphere. Gus waved his hand to the Rangers outside and backed up. They shot him simultaneously in the head 8 times. Brain matter got on Gus's blue and yellow jacket, he just wiped it off and felt like crying. It was over and he didn't stop him, what a failure he would be known as this all started to sink in.

The first time America has ever been bombed in mass scale on it's soil. They ran down the stairs and relayed the info to the men. Everyone's hearts were demolished, obliterated, needless to say all of their families and friends back home. They went to the Hummers and Gus got in the back door and sat next to Charles Jones shaking his head.

"We did it." Charles said motioning to his screen.

Gus was just about in tears thinking about everyone back home. "What are you talking about? It already happened. I saw Mustafa press the button, I saw it on the screen, mushroom clouds all over the US. Millions are already dead."

"Silly goose, I disabled that detonator about an hour ago. I tried calling you, but nothing went through. He must have jammed our comm system. And that must have just been a simulation that you saw on the screen because here is the last 24 hours of weather over the US, not a cloud in the sky. We did it."

"So the nukes didn't go off?"

"No, I told you I already had that damn thing found and disabled. All over the internet. Pretty cool huh?"

"Oh thank God, Thank God for you Charles. You are the best."

"You're not so bad yourself there Rogers."

Chapter 22

CIA Headquarters New York

They were in Sarah's office watching it all on the screens and when Jones disabled the detonator a gasp was let out by Christie and Alfie clapped in jubilation. "Thank God for Jones, man is he good."

Sarah was busy on her laptop and said, "That's what we train them to do."

Alfie responded back, "Something makes me think that they didn't train him to do all that. That was know how and instincts."

"Maybe so but we have jumpers that have to take control of 33 more tankers before we are totally out of the clear."

Christie was an eager beaver, "Hurry and switch back to the tankers, I want to see how we're doing out there."

"Okay, okay." Sarah promptly changed the CIA channels with a different tanker on each screen. They all watched intently and discussed what they were seeing.

Christie saw the resistance to some of the jumpers that were attempting to take control of one of the tankers. "What if the men on the ships are Mustafa's men?"

"As you saw in the last video not even the Sheik knew about what Mustafa had done."

"What about the standoff on the Houston tanker?" Alfie interjected.

Sarah now rethought her opinion, "You know what you might be right, Mustafa could have had some of his Al-Qeada chronies put on board. This could get ugly."

Alfie had some other thoughts, "If those nukes go off this could be a catastrophe worse than the Valdez and BP oil spill combined. This could be disastrous for the environment as well."

"If those nukes go off sharks and dolphins aren't going to be the only ones getting killed. And that's what we should be more concerned with right now." Sarah said flipping to another channel.

Christie wanted to know, "Has Obama gone on TV to tell those people to get out of those cities yet?"

Sarah realized that they were in that group. "Those cities? New York will be one of the main targets. What the heck are we still doing here?"

Alfie had some logic to the Presidents decision. "With only a few hours notice it would cause more panic than progress to get out. There wouldn't be enough time to get out. The closer they get, the further the blast zone gets. All of New York City would be blown off the map."

"Speaking of the blast radius has Kerry said what kind of nukes they are?"

"Right, if they are cluster or titan nukes the blast radius could be much further inland than just one bomb."

"The entire east and west coastline could be vapor."

"I'll call Kerry." Sarah said picking up her cell phone. "Kerry, hey what kind of nukes are we talking about here?"

"Houston nuke was just a standard nuke however, the one headed toward Seattle that we just dismantled was a Titan."

"Any news on the one headed our way?"

"Nope I'll let you know as soon as we get to it."

"Thanks."

Sarah hung up and started talking to Christie and Alfie, "Some are normal and some are Titans, there is no telling what is headed to New York."

"Can you bring up the New York team?"

"Yeah, just a minute." Sarah took the remote and a swig of coffee and flipped until they saw the team on the tanker.

"Wait, this one says Boston."

2nd Class Lt. Sandra James, US Air Force, had her sniper rifle poised, perched 50 yards away from the control tower of the crane operator. They had just chuted on board the ship and one of her crew mates had just been hit in a skirmish between the Al-Qaeda rebels. She helped him over to a safe zone and grabbed his rifle, and climbed to a distant peak on some containers to take out the operator. This would allow Captain

Waylon Wheaton access to climb on top of the containers and disarm the nuclear weapon. Captain Waylon had a device that detected Uranium on a FOLED gui screen made by Universal Display given to him for this specific mission.

Waylon was at the base of the containers and waiting on Sandra to finish the bastard off. Meanwhile inside the control tower there were several men inside pointing this way and that as the operator methodically moved the containers to jumble up the mix so that the Air Force personnel couldn't find the weapon. Waylon had to run about the deck of the ship several times to escape the containers that were being dropped overhead in his direction.

Sandra on the other hand had complexities and dilemma's all of her own. The control tower had bullet proof glass and she was currently in the process of notching out a hole around the direct path from where she was to the place where the operator was standing. She thought that if she fired enough in the same spot that she could get through the third world country manufactured bullet-proof glass. With each squeeze of the trigger it made a muffled noise as the muzzle had a silencer attached. Her scope was wide with cross hairs that were extremely narrow and thin, each with notches of degrees lining the vertical line of the cross hairs.

Nathan was the sniper of the group, but he was too badly injured to do any good right now so it was up to her and her minimal training in the art that would get them all out of this mess. She recalled all of her brief training in sniper school, which was really, a one day thing. Their main thing was kind of like a fire alarm use only in case of emergency. Well the alarm bar had been pulled and it was her time to shine.

The crane operator moved a container to the base where Waylon was and as usual Waylon checked it and, "Bingo, Eureka I have found one for the Queen, I shall surely be knighted." Waylon spoke into his talker that Sandra heard and radioed back.

"Roger that, firing now, get on that thing and get inside." Sandra said as she confidently squeezed the trigger. "Zzzffftt." Direct hit, theory proven , it works, her bullet went all the way through the other bullet in the glass.

"Operator down, I got him, now get in there and disarm that thing." Sandra said as she observed the scene inside the tower. The bullet nailed the rebel but just after that another crane operator jumped over at the controls and pushed the dead rebel aside.

Captain Waylon climbed atop the container and started working on his torch to cut out a way to get inside. Just as he made it to the top of the container the operator picked it up and it ascended into the air and Waylon clutched on for dear life. He was tossed to the edge and grabbed on to a loop and latched his belt on it and went swinging at its side. He was safe, and screaming all the way. Sandra got the point and zeroed in through the cross hairs at the next idiot rebel.

"Hang in there Captain I'll have you down from there in just a minute, give me one chance..."

The turban freak was right inside the T she squeezed and, "Zzzffft."

"Another dead Rebel." Sandra said, as Waylon reached for his radio tethered to his belt.

"My goodness, how many more are there? I can't take much more of this." Waylon said with his back to the ground floor deck swinging on the side of the container.

"I am doing my best, I think there is one more to go. As soon as he steps up to the plate I'll take him out."

The Afghan rebel had no intention of getting on the controls and hid just below the edge of the window. Sandra spotted him and never being dull she said to Waylon, "This bastard doesn't want to die, but die he must. I'll find a way you hang on there buddy."

Sandra zeroed in on his face just between his eyes, she yanked back on the trigger and, "Zzzffftt." The rebel shot up out of there as he followed the bullet straight into the glass just in front of him. After that close call he bolted out of there and went out the back door. Sandra knew that she had to do something, that rebel was the only one left after the skirmish and he must die or be put down.

She climbed down and gave the rifle to Nathan the wounded one and said, "Fire if you get a shot."

"Will do." Nathan gathered himself and got into a position to where he could see one area of the tower.

"Cover me!" Sandra shouted dismounting the container down to the deck.

Taking ginger steps she took her side arm 9mm and held it with both hands. Slowly she made her way up to the steps and began to climb with one free hand with pistol ready. In the meantime Waylon climbed up on top of the now steady container and started cutting with his torch. Sandra made it to the top of the steps and secured the tower. She went around to the back door which was already open and got the controls of the crane and lowered it down to the deck of the ship.

Waylon finally cut a good sized hole in the top of it and proceeded into the dark hole. When his boots hit the container floor he got out a 40,000 candle lite power flashlight and positioned it so he could go to work. After a few minutes he was inside the packaging and torching his way through the missile.

Sandra now was strafing her way around the sides of the tower looking for the rebel. She went around to the back and saw someone in a brown shirt headed back into the control room in the front door. She quickly swifted around to the door, which was locked so she blasted it with the 9mm. It swung open and she crouched readying her gun searching for the rebel.

While Sandra was doing this the rebel had hoisted the container back into the air and Sandra heard Waylon shouting inside the container as she turned to look it was coming right at her. She jumped out of the way and the container hit the railing of the walkway. When it hit one of the cables broke and Waylon went shifting inside to one corner and fell off the nuke packaging.

The rebel crane operator swung it back to hit the other containers and then another cable snapped and Waylon landed with his back to the side of the container. Just as the packaged nuke went sliding towards him he jumped out of the way and it hit the side. Right after the container hit the operator shifted the controls to make it move back towards the railing.

Sandra saw where it was going and she sprinted to the doorway and into the control room shooting her way in. One of the bullets hit the rebel in the leg and he dropped his gun on the floor. Sandra went straight for the levers and pushed it back to a neutral position then jumped on the floor for the gun. The rebel attained the gun in the fight and she grabbed hold of the gun and when he put his finger under the trigger she pushed it above them and a shot went off.

Sandra backed away and the bullet ricocheted around the metal inside the room and hit the rebel in the chest just as he was aiming it at her. She then fired a few rounds into his chest and the rebel let loose of his gun.

The container with Waylon in it hit the side railing and jolted him towards the other side. Sandra then took control of the levers and moved the container back to the deck ship floor. Quickly she ran outside and down the steps to the hole in the container and yelled into it, "Are you alright?"

Shaken up some Waylon responded, "I think so. I have to disarm this thing and quick we are getting closer to the mainland."

"I don't think that the rebels will be bothering us anymore so get after it if you can."

"Okay." Waylon slowly made his way over to the flashlight and positioned it over his work area and went in with the clippers. A few snips later it was disarmed and a helicopter had just arrived to pick them up.

Chapter 24

ATLANTIC WATERS

100 miles off the coast of New York City

The aircrtaft carriers werc in hot pursuit and had the New York oil tanker in its sights ahead on the horizon. They were heading due east and Captain Jordan Pressley was at the helm, towards the North he spotted a small ship that was traveling at high speeds back toward the mainland. Lt. Commander Jeremy Robinson noticed through his binoculars that the ship was unmarked and they discarded it as just another boat.

Lt. Commander Robinson said, "Just a sea vessel, nothing with terra oil on it sir."

"Is the team ready to board?" Captain Pressley wanted to know as he took the binoculars from Robinson and viewed the ship in the distance.

"Yes sir."

"Very good." The ship had now passed their position to the North of them and the Captain lost sight of the vessel.

When they arrived at the tanker there was a team of rebels that were there to greet them. Ensign Holly Whitehurst was the first of the Navy SEALs to board. She spoke decently in standard arabic and when standing face to face with their leader she asked, "Tell me where the bomb is."

The arab dressed in white said, "What bomb?"

Holly yelled back to the men, "We are going to have to find it on our own. Get everyone up here now."

Seal team 4 all boarded the tanker and immediately went for the containers. Each had their detectors in hand and was surveying each container quite fast. The detector was a hand held device that could search for all types of nukes with the selection on the OLED screen. They searched for Uranium, Hydrogen, Plutonium, HMX, octogen, Beryllium, Tritium – Dueterium and all of the various components of a nuke.

Holly was already up on a container and had the detector programmed to detect all of the known components..., "Nothing, I haven't found a thing."

Seal Jonathan Beard was finding the same thing on his detector, "Keep trying, it's gotta be here somewhere."

As Holly was climbing to another container with Kennedy Cooke helping her up, she latched on to the top of a green container and got a hand full of grease. She let go and landed down on the container below and said, "Okay, Kennedy lift me up over here."

He pushed and she was atop and already scanning. Kennedy secured his detector and not wanting to find grease again he positioned himself to the side and took a running start and jumped, making his way up to where Holly was.

Holly was kind of the ringleader of the whole bunch and she was wondering if anyone had found it yet. She went to the edge of the container and yelled out to everyone, "Has everyone scanned their containers?"

They all said intermittently, " Yeah, we got nothing."

Kenned did the last scan and clipped his detector to his belt and said, "We scanned all of them and we got nothing, sweet momma."

"I think it's time that we talk to our Arab Afghan friends." Holly said jumping down to the deck of the ship. She then lead the way as the others followed her to the control room. There the little beady eyed towel heads were laughing it up.

Holly climbed the stairs and could hear them laughing accompanied by the smell of the ocean. Her look was harsh and stern like a vice-principal about to give some licks or dish out some punishment. The Seal team backed her and stood directly behind her as they saw the look on Holly's face the Afghans got real quiet.

Without any hesitation Holly started, "What's so funny you evil towel heads? Know something that we don't?"

Jabeeb the Captain of the tanker got a serious look on his face as well and said, "It is nothing we were just telling jokes."

"Do you think it's funny? You better not." Then she got her 9mm. Out and shot him in the leg. "Now that's blood and if you keep bleeding you will die. Now is it still funny?"

"You crazy woman."

"That's nothing compared to what I'll do if you don't tell me where the nuke is. Now talk."

"You shot me."

"Yeah and next time it will be your brains leaking out onto your clothes or on the clothes of your friends if you don't talk."

"I know nothing." How to get them to talk? There are several ways really, and if none of them work I'll be put on some reality TV show or selling meatballs on QVC. This was their time, their jaunt away from the usual dog and pony show of just training and going through routines. There could be only one way to get these mindless curry freaks to talk.

"Can you guess what my last name is?"

"No. What is it?"

Holly Whitehurst quickly shot him in the face and his brains went splattering all over his friends behind him. "I won't even give you the luxury of that. Someone throw his body over board."

Another one of the Afghan rebels said, "Holy shit, you are out of your mind." Of course in the usual scared of your, peeing in your pants, turban for brains, mind accent.

"I will be more than happy to take your life too there towel head, if you don't tell me where the bomb is." She enunciated those last words very distinctly to enforce her power over them as she grabbed the man's shirt and brought it close to her face.

"Okay, okay just don't shoot." Yeah don't shoot I don't even know God yet and I like warm sunny places like exotic beaches, but burning in hell for an eternity isn't my idea of a vacation from this pathetic life.

"Now you're oh, so willing to talk?"

"The ship left here about twenty minutes ago it is headed straight to New York it has the nuke." Yeah, unfortunately it took a mind blowing use of brute force to get these rag heads to say anything other than, yeah I like mustard and I guess I like biscuits too. With curry on top of course.

Holly looked to the team and said, "We gotta go. Head out." Like a baby that had been plucked from heaven and sent on a journey that would last a lifetime to figure out that you're really not alone in this world, or the next.

They jumped back on the aircraft carrier and she told Captain Pressley what the Afghan said. Yeah, the Pete and Repeat bar scene once again.

His response was, "I saw that ship as we were approaching the tanker. Yall need to get on the Seal Delivery boat. It will be much faster." Now there's an idea, speed, wind in your hair as you travel across miles of ocean to find some psychopath waiting to kill you.

"Right on." They had been trained by other dog and pony shows to do the very thing that they were seeking to avoid. Death by a curry stained hand squeezing the trigger of a gun that Osama bought from Iraq.

"Any means necessary." What he was really saying was sure they are all expendable, the towel head psychopaths that is, and please don't use discretion in which one you splatter brain matter on first.

"Got it, we're out." Out on a mission that red tape wouldn't allow them to write home to mommy and daddy from summer camp about.

They all piled into the Seal delivery boat which was equipped with weapons and various scuba accessories. All that they would need was on their boat so it dropped with a splash and they were moving out towards the west.

Ahh, the open sea and salt water in your mouth gave rise to some serious reflection. Holly wanted to motivate the men before they stormed the hospital shooting everyone in their path to perform open heart surgery on an explosive device. Holly said loudly, "As Oprah Winfrey once said, "My philosophy is that you are not only responsible for your life, but doing the best at this moment puts you in the best place for the next moment."

This pretty much summarized what they were doing now and what they were about to do in a carpenters way of avoiding the countless pints of blood that could be used for research. Who wants to work on a Terrorist cadaver anyway? The best terrorist anyway, is a dead one. No research or polls conducted were to be needed to figure out the heart of an American President.

After all this dinner for shmucks blasting of brain matter that was about to take place wasn't an invitation only thing. Who invited these vermin to ruin 9 million dinners in New York on a perfectly democraticly fine dining night in America. Osama Bin Laden might have invited them but he would not be around to see his loyal freakshow Afghans die. And that was too bad really, for him not to see that some red blooded Americans could out think his heinous insipid terrorist mind was really a shame.

The delivery boat finally caught up with the terrorists and the SEAL team was more than ready for action. Kevin Abtak had his Mk 18 readied, that's the standard issue of machine guns that the Navy Seal's use these days. He saw no signs of life on board the ship that had suddenly come to a halt. The Seal team K-bar task-force delivery boat was tied off on the terrorist ship and just when Kevin Abtak was about to board the ship one of the Afghan's popped their head out from around a corner and started firing at him. He fired back and hit the bastard right in the chest as he went to the floor.

Kevin was thinking that he was in the clear so he stepped on board when another Afghan rebel came out from around the same corner and shot Kevin in the gut. He went toppling overboard and immediately Jonathan Beard fired back and shot the rebel in the face.

Naturally all of them rushed over to Kevin to pull him out of the water. There was no reason for him to die from a shark wound or an eel shock if he only got shot in the gut, Holly figured. Arm in arm, Jonathan was leaning over into the rift on the side of the skiff's rubber casing, grabbing Kevin. Once he was back on board the crew saw the blood gushing out of his stomach area.

Jonathan had regrets, "Damn it, I should have had you covered."

Kevin spoke up in response, "I sent her an email just in case." It was all that he could say or think about. This is modern days, and no he didn't have some letter tucked away in one of his pouches to give whoever made it back.

Jonathan remained positive, "You'll see her again."

Kevin said, "It's cold." Yeah, about as cold as a dying polar bear that had just been hunted down by a terrorist eskimo.

"Get him dry and warm." Kennedy was the first to reach in his pack and get out his blanket. Holly had a towel and dried his shoulders and then used it to put pressure on his wound.

They were all pretty much ducked down attending to Kevin hovering over the dying Seal when some shots rang out over his head. Jonathan still had his Mk 18 around his shoulder and slung it around then popped up and shot another terrorist just before he jumped aboard. "Freaking kama kazi terrorists, well meet allah aka hell."

The dark faced bearded rebel fell in the rift. Holly saw another one of them peering out from behind the side of the ship, "There's more of them, Jonathan, Colt go, Kennedy and I will take care of Kevin."

The said men arose, armed and jumped over to the rebel ship like they were going in for a dunk. There was a cabin below deck where they were all coming out of, and Jonathan got the idea to throw a grenade into the depths. He yanked the clip out and threw the thing in there. A few seconds later they heard the explosion and many yells, as smoke came billowing out.

They stood at the entrance and waited for the smoke to clear when a terrorist came running out firing so they both went to each side, bailing for it. They didn't have time to shoot and the rebel made it all the way to the back of the ship and pushed a container over board. The rebel had no chance and yelled out with fists in the air and a smile that kills, "For Allah! For Allah!"

Now that was unusual, then it hit them as the fired on the defenseless bastard and he went toppling over the back of the ship. Colt immediately went back over to their skiff and packed on his scuba gear without saying a word and in no time he was going backwards into the Atlantic. He was already wearing his wet suit and took some deep breaths into the twin hose setup mouthpiece. Peering out over the sides they just saw bubbles arising.

Colt kicked vigorously until he saw the container plummeting into the depths. He checked his gage, 100 ft, more breaths and strong kicks. He was closing in on it as his flashlight on his diving mask searched into the void and streamed to a dull gray box kept its descent. Following after it further he reached 150 ft. and took more breaths in his mouthpiece. He said a quick prayer, still plummeting, mask first arms at his side, shoulders swiveling, he descended further.

He had been trained to go to these depths, but had only done it in controlled environments, this would put his training to the test. He began to gain on the box with every kick of his fins. Suddenly it stopped with debris flying upward, he was in a cloud. Quickly he kicked in the opposite direction then hit the container with his legs and part of a fin. He stood on the ocean floor now 200ft. below the surface eyes on the cloud around him as sediment arose from his landing. He swept with his hands to clear the debris and got a clean path of vision.

The container's dimensions were about 6' x 3' rectangle shaped, he had to cut through the exterior. Behind his twin tank setup was his pack that he reached around and pulled off. With torch in hand he cut along the top edges, slowly he made it through the metal. The brightness of the torch made sunspots in his vision, he kept going, avoiding looking directly at it.

Sea creatures were swimming about him, he paid no attention. Finally the scorched line of his torch came back around to where he had started and shoved the top away from himself. Colt now had a look at what was in the container, one streamdlined missile. He cut through the outer casing and found ten separate canisters wrapped around a central core, and proceeded to cut through the first one. Wires, he reached back and got the snips from his pack. He knew his stuff and clipped the first wire, nothing, and that was a good sign. Now he just had to repeat it nine times.

Slowly he made his way through the next several clips, it was smooth sailing. Finally he got to the last casing and flipped it up to see the wires, in his mind he thought, clip this last one and he could be on the surface in a minute. His snips were in his right hand and he steadied his position on the wire opening the clippers as the jaws of the clippers were ready for the snip.

Just as he made a move towards the wire, through his mask, he saw something coming right at him, white teeth lunging right at him.

On the surface Holly was watching as Kevin's eyes went blank. They had already left the ship behind and were traveling back to the aircraft carrier. They had called in the coast guard for Colt and a helicopter would be arriving shortly.

Kevin died and Holly said to Jonathan, "As C.S. Lewis once said, Has the world been so kind to you that you should leave it with regret, there are better things ahead than any that we leave behind."

Just then their skiff started gaining on the aircraft carrier in the distance as a huge wave began forming behind them. Holly looked back and saw in the distance a huge mushroom of water emerging from the surface then retracting. "Colt! He didn't make it." She wept and Jonathan offered his shoulder and hugged her as she began to soak the shoulder of his coat.

"It's okay Holly, its just as you have said, he is in a better place, there are better things ahead of him."

The wave generated from the explosion propelled the skiff into the aircraft carrier. Holly looked back and saw the Coast Guard that would have been rescuing Colt going towards them.

Chapter 25

LEXINGTON KENTUCKY, MITCH McCONNEL'S OFFICE

After the news of the final bomb being detonated Air Force One landed in Lexigton Kentucky and President Barak Obama made their way into Mitch McConnel's office. Mitch McConnel was the leading Republican on the Senate and held the position of Senate Minority leader. They all setup shop for a Presidential Address as the news teams made their way into the office.

With the Presidential seal behind him he stepped up to the podium and spoke, "Citizens of the United States it is with much sadness and relief that I am coming to you with tonight. Let me start off with telling you of the reason for my relief and gratitude. Approximately two and a half hours ago we received information that thirty-four oil tankers were headed to every major port city of the United States. These tankers were all armed with nuclear explosives and the terrorists were aboard those tankers were instructed to detonate each bomb when arriving at their destination."

"I can thankfully say that with the help of our gifted Armed Forces, and loyal men and women in service to this great country, not one of the oil tankers actually made it to their intended destinations. All of the nuclear weapons were disarmed before they could make it to the ports. Regretfully one of those warheads was detonated about 50 miles off the coast of New York City. There were no damages and New York only experienced a slight earthquake due to the explosion."

"I would personally like to extend my condolences to the family of Colt Shipley US Navy Seal who was responsible for disarming nine of the ten nukes on the Titan missile. Unfortunately his life was taken in the process as he was over 200 ft below the Atlantic disarming the bomb, if it were not for his courage and bravery all of New York would have been demolished. He never gave up and never quit, down to the last weapon."

"In addition I would like to thank all of the teams of the Air Force who were successful in disarming 33 of the other nuclear weapons. Our Armed Forces played instrumental roles today and as Americans we can never thank them enough for what they have done for their country. Our men and women of service ensure and protect our freedoms that we relish so dearly today, if it were not for them we would not be the country that we are today."

"Today was have triumphed over the evils of the terrorist world and today one of our Army Ranger teams went out into the night and were successful in killing the leader of the Al-Qaeda network, Mustafa Hasbaland. The war on terror, this week alone, has seen both of the leaders of Al-Qaeda including Osama Bin Laden put to justice. In closing, I encourage you, every time that you see a member of our Armed Forces that you go up and thank them for their service. We owe them so much and the least we can do is show our gratitude. Thank you and good night America."

Chapter 26

CHRISTIE'S APARTMENT, NEW YORK 9:06 PM

After the President's speech Christie invited Alfie over for a movie just to relax and get their mind off the last few weeks. Christie was also hoping for some romance that she had been seeking and seeing in the words and actions of Alfie over the last few days. They were now closer than ever and pretty much inseparable, so it was only rational that they end up holding hands on Christie's couch.

Just before they put in the movie they were watching The Bachelorette and Alfie said, "There she is, remember in Afghanistan I was saying that you looked like her."

"Who Alfie?"

"Ali Fedotowski, The Bachelorette."

"She's gorgeous, I don't think I am that pretty."

"You are and even more so."

"Thank you, that's sweet."

"You're sweet."

"Oh, stop it."

"No, you are, you noticed that the tanker said Sasawaha."

"Sasawaha? I think you just like saying that word."

"How sweet is that? You saved us, the US, from being bombed now really, how sweet is that? And you took a chance on this lonely programmer, sweetest woman in the world."

"Thank you." She then snuggled in closer and put the popcorn on the other side of them for better romantic situations. She grabbed the remote and hit the close button and the previews began. They watched as the Transformers came to Earth, Mark Zuckerberg programmed Facebook, and King George the sixth learn how to talk like a royal. By the time the King was sounding out consonants and vowels with his mouth, Christie had her mouth tangled around Alfie's interlocked in a passionate kiss. The lobby music of the movie just played on as there was to be no pressing of the play button only unbuttoning of Christie's blouse, a much anticipated release.

Christie then said, "So much for taking it slow."

And with that release there was much excitement on the red carpet as the greats prepared to go inside the theater. Once they were inside the theater and in a cush surrounding, The Aviator took the show as clothes turned into airplanes and they went soaring about the screen. Next on tap was The Firm as Christie grabbed the legal ledger and went to work. Finally there was Spy Game as Brad Pitt went undercover in a vast network of assassins to save the woman of his dreams. And as Alfie saved her she saved him right back with a kiss.

Alfie remembered that Christie usually liked to take things one rose at a time and with all of his clothes off he couldn't reach his phone. Christie then held up her silk panties which had a beautiful rose on the front of them and she said, "One rose at a time."

Alfie just smiled and waited for the climax of the movie to begin. Thus was French Kiss as Meg Ryan agreed to buy the necklace. For the stare up at the ceiling for the both of them, Meg and Luc made warm feelings of starting a vineyard together in France.

As tired as they were they went to sleep in each others arms. Morning came and Alfie was in the kitchen making breakfast for Christie when her phone began to ring. Christie answered it, "Hello?"

"Christie, this is Kerry."

"Is everything okay?"

"Yes and no, there has been an incident."

"What happened?"

"We found Osama Bin Laden, and he's alive."

"I thought they found his body in the Afghan cave."

"No that wasn't him, what we did find though was pictures from one of my agents in Somalia. Pictures of Osama in Sasawaha after he was thought to be dead. Then this morning an agent in Paris ran a facial point check on a subway camera and who do you think it was?"

"Osama?"

"Yeah, only now he is clean cut and in a business suit."

"Is there anything we can do?"

"I need you and Alfie to go to Paris and meet up at our headquarters there where you will be briefed on your mission."

Alfie called out from the kitchen, "Honey, who is it?"

Christie yelled back, "It's Kerry."

"Tell him I said hi."

Kerry resumed the conversation, "Your tickets are paid for as well as your suite at the hotel, call me if you have any more questions."

"Okay, we will."

"Goodbye."

"Honey!" Christie yelled into the kitchen.

"Yes." Alfie stood at her door with a tray of food on it.

"I talked to Kerry and we're going to Paris."

"That's great. What for?"

"Osama is alive."

"Really...great. I mean great we're finally going to Paris."